This book is dedicated to Julia and the International
Illuminatus Conspiracy.

Pulp Books
is an imprint of Pulp Faction
PO Box 12171, London N19 3HB
First published 1997 by Pulp Books
All rights reserved

Come is a work of fiction. Any character
resemblance to people living or dead is
purely coincidental

A CIP record for this book is available
from the British Library
ISBN 1 901072 010
CD Edition ISBN 1 901072 037
(A limited edition of 750 copies)

Cover design by Engine
Cover photography by Julia King
Typeset by Crash Composition
(UK) Ltd, Liverpool, England

c o m e

a novel by Mark Waugh

To Kat

More queen ?

love Mark

Acknowledgment.
From the masterplan to the mastermix has been a long
and enlightening process. I would like to thank all of
those who have either worked on or been inspirational
in the creation of *Come*.

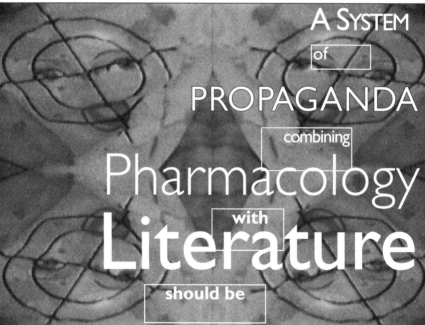

"I am a

non-sexual

being"

Jeff Stryker
The Face June 1993

A SYSTEM

of

PROPAGANDA

combining

Pharmacology

with

Literature

should be

completely and infallibly effective"
Aldous Huxley
The Olive Tree

The ear is an open vein. Knowledge is a drug. To start the story now when the batteries are so low. As the winter closes in and the books come out.

Every horizon is obsolete.

This story would be easier to tell if I hadn't already tampered with the text. Like a lover I worked with the words until their meaning was mined and gushed its lubricant into fecundity. The dirt on the disk has consumed that passion. Time seals the tombs of the Pharaohs. The crimes of the future are taught in the past. Love is a corpse wrapped in transparent plastic.

So now you know nothing of the story that hides behind this fog in an ocean of translucent words.

So now you read the letters C-O-M-E with cruel indifference, and who knows what special effects raise this machine from the dead.

So know you now both coda and the tail?

Words are mnemonic equations that derail the senses as they track a world that disappears before them. In books words convey cultural traffic across invisible borders. Words are signs that lead us astray.

Chapter <1>
Mnemonic Fetishes

Qanguage helps us remember the equation of DNA. It is a surface nexus of variable density. I began to write a story about the seductive depth of the smile. The smile particular to a digitized image. This is the story that lost the plot. What remains is the fiendish glimmer of an emerging story: a stroke of genius and the strophe of representation.

⑨

"No Mona, no more!" The voice screams down the telephone.

I am telling you a story.

I haven't told you before?

"It seems very real. It's not a true story?"

"Forget it—I'll phone back later…"

Where was i. In the lower case already, spiralling down into the infinity of the origin, the *fort da*, the joy of departing returns, the deja vu of narration in this mise en scene of seduction. It begins with beginnings and ends in the cut: the perverse incision into the universal trade between cultures. This culture is an organic equation. I drift with galleons laden with treasure across familiar Tropics.

The ocean is space.

Undulating waves of differentials. Mystical transportations converge in the ear. Gold, spice, slaves and technologies are traded for power in the smooth voice of a media mercenary.

The phone rings, interrupting the sentence.

"Hello? Yes. Yes. No. Don't ask. I have the notebooks and the file but the computer reads:

Error in document edit.

"This absolute disruption of the surface leaves me confused but it's true that the images of the original haunt me. I am always ready to puncture myself and let a bit of the spirit of LSM into the day. The book exists only as a nexus for nostalgic cartographies."

"Wasn't it about an inflatable doll?"

"Yes."

"I told you the story last year?"

"Yeah, so what?"

It is a simple story, set between Brighton, London and Paris. An English text with French subtitles. A love story. The story of Dolly Savage, inflatable woman. The memoirs of a prophylactic interface between subjectivity and seriality, surrealism and sensationalism, a ribbed invagination and artificial insemination. She had a genius for melodrama and a penchant for: Stentorphone, pretty ethnics, guns, Gucci, Garage, bondage, psychoactive nutrients, deviant mail-order mags, Manga video, and perpetual access to excess.

It began as an idea to recontextualise Freud's Psychobiography of Leonardo, a witty and deceitful intrigue that manifested itself as the film, *Leonardo Seduce Me*, codified *LSM* or *Come*.

Blurring the boundaries between truth and fiction, I babble into the receiver about the exchange between film and painting, invoking animated drawings by Natalia. My words mould themselves with shrinkwrap tenacity to the invention of a context for my psychosis.

"Simulation is upon us when we believe in pure transcendent categories—God, genius, Man—the dream has us in its bind..." Perhaps I'm losing them; I throw in some salacious gossip:

"Leonardo was a well-dressed fashionable Adonis with a penchant for sodomy and decapitation..."

This is a looped soundbyte with a funky beat behind it. A perverse impulse sets the rhythm. Between monologue and dialogue is the ellipsis of communication. The weird waves between us.

I hang up, tired by this repetition, by the trivia that has besieged my story. I knew that my flight of rhetoric had been decrypted by their spies. The telephone is a double agent.

Words are mnemonic configurations of letters that remind us of a sound. Speech remembers the perversity of disconnection...

I forgot that you have already heard this and dub the English version with more Italian.

As the page becomes warmer I forget about the telephone messages, the stories that are enveloping the trajectory of DS. A body drifting fascinated by the distortion of the mirror. The perfect calligraphic inversion that binds the reflections of the Renaissance to this

s p a c e d

o   u   t

zone

system

and its rigid architecture between the original and the copy.

Leonardo filled his notebooks with observations of perverse and universal insight. Accounts and failed projects... the mysterious line of the creative genesis, the fragmentation of the pedagogy in the ascent of the individual, from bit part in Vasari to centre stage in the genealogy of the War Machine.

Come is the title of the book that Dolly is reading. Mark called her DS for short. DS is a stranger sometimes. She reads while others talk. She is listening to what they say and mixing their narratives with her own. She slips into the words on the page and draws you into the lubricated text.

She reads on the train from Brighton to London. She reads to disappear.

She stands on the tube from Victoria to Charing Cross. The date is October 1988. Culture is a flashback to the evolution of discourse.

DS is on MDMA.

Å

Heaven is a nightclub surrounded by whores and dropouts. History is a memory cell overloaded with fashion tips.

DS. She's not Slack. She comes out when you are depressed. She loves dance music and the underground vibe. She is an anonymous part of the crowd. She waves her hands in the air and belongs to infinity. When the price is right she'll score E's for her mates. Dealing in clubs makes her feel nervous. Even dummies sometimes confess.

In the nineties, history, like many disciplines that evolved in the nineteenth century, had only a vague popular meaning. In the secret files of the universities other schematic paradigms were being written. DS is a member of a cult that future historians might describe as encapsulating the era. She is a pleasure-seeking miscreant totally clued-up on the capital tip. Spinning around the club scene like a ball on a roulette wheel, she unloads her stock and networks a niche. Everyone likes to gamble and as MC Kinky said, "Everything starts with an E."

MDMA is a psychotropic drug. It makes you smile. DS loves the way she feels as the code pulses through her. She loves the energy of the other dancers.

On this particular October night, DS is rushing off her tits and standing in line with the others.

The nightclub is the airport terminus of the pleasure principle. Travellers are body-searched as they have little luggage. One is rarely strip-searched in clubs. The imagination is a warped machine.

The truth is never chic.

Dreams of flight are thought to be sexual. The dream declares a desire to transgress, to break with gravity, to scribble wings and become animal. Freud saw in Leonardo's helicopter drawings a new model for biographical writing.

Bouncers reassure the punters with a whisper,

"It's alright, we're looking for weapons."

Drugs confiscated are like metaphysical theorems, they reappear in parallel dimensions, causing confused euphoria. DS is a transparent diffuser of the pharmakon. A molotov of memories and laughter. She moves through Heaven with petrochemical allure. Several exposures are rendered obsolete by the virtual confessions of Cyberpunks but you remember the look. The sensation of the *realthing*, body and soul on a trajectory of impulsive nihilism. Sex and Text: *Technosex*, analogue angels squirm in genital meltdown, solder trickles across the synapses.

The DJ is psychoactive, rewording the connections that have relapsed. The body responds to his biogenetic precision, as if possessed by a Loa of the Voodoo cult.

Magical electricity conspires in Heaven, lights and projections detail the surface. Jeff Koons says that God is in the details. Artists like quoting artists. The image is a stroboscopic effect of a body without organs. A transgressive fiction of escape routes and a pharmacopia for cool mediums of knowledge.

The split-screen was used in silent movies to infer the unfolding of time in multiple space. In *The Birth of Tragedy*, the young philologist, F Nieztsche, unravelled a dionysian future for music. The story is an obsolete perversion. A fetish of tongues. The silent version of Jekyll and Hyde used the spider as a metaphor for schizophrenia. It is an organism of multiple perspectives.

DS is a drug to facilitate multiple orgasms.

Å

"I imagine the story orbiting me. He wrote this story about a sex toy. One of those gross mail order items. He's a real sick fuck. You know that the Japanese are into those inflatable dolls. I saw them in a magazine called *Flash*. Salarymen will part with a lot of Yen for a smooth-seamed model!"

"People don't talk about 'smooth-seamed models' they talk about TV!"

"So what?"

"So who's going to talk about DS?"

"Everyone talks about DS,
   Everyone is on line with the code,
   Everyone is ready to switch sides,
   Everyone is ready to become the other.
   Everyone is perversely predatory."

DS is on the dancefloor. Everyone is dancing and sweating. Functional semiotics of bodies in rapture. She sees her fuck dancing with some boys. She moves towards her...

Å

The film jumps in the gate. The scene shudders, DS is in a flashback. A virginal time of slow striptease. The event is formatted and the digits logged.

BRIGHTON BEACH AT SUNRISE

Mouth to minge beneath the ruined pier.

Cliches of erotic desire.

THE YELLOW FACE OF

The sunflower climbing like Icarus into the warm currents of heliotropic myth.

The raw and exposed wound of the Vietnamese girl, scarred in eternity by the ejaculation of US desire...

THE VOICE OF

California in the haze of Napalm and grammatological warfare, the virus of thought in the libidinal trace.

The smile stops here.

Å

The smile still floats victoriously over devastation and decay, as though it could endure a thousand deaths. Is sex not a memory of le

petit mort, the merged texture of incomprehensible strokes? A sacrifice of names in the silent choreography of tongues?

Marcel Duchamp added a moustache to the Mona Lisa, and a new name, *L.H.O.O.Q.* Pronounced in French this might translate as, "She has a hot bit of tail!"

Culture is a drug that destroys the pleasure principle. Dealing death to those who accelerate beyond its ancient gearing system. The pleasure principle destroys itself as it becomes culture. Language is the hallucinogenic medium that destroys its creators in a thirst for exquisite configurations of meaning. *Everything starts with an Edit.* Models fall from glossy magazines into the book, their lines are cut by phantoms. I bring down the BPMs of my syllable, saturated, sentences to match the timbre of, *La Carte Postale.* Sweating with hyperaesthesia I cut my story with surface mystery and stereo atmospherics.

Å

The story is destroyed by a psychotropic cocktail.

"I'd forgotten a lot of this."

"I told you that he used a combination of the hypnotic, Diorden and the narcotic analgesic opiate, Codeine. This set metabolises as a morphine like opiate that works similarly to endorphins."

"So DS is Jewish and likes E. Am I missing something essential to the economy of this story?"

"No. Freud is Jewish, Marx is Jewish, my lover is Jewish. DS is serious product."

"I think of her as a Rubik cube. A twentieth century toy and receptacle of love. A station for thought that has no home, an uncanny and difficult axis that baffles and delights us. The *fort da* of the computer game, the acceleration of difference in the field of information, the logic and brutality of reason, a nexus of sensuality and plasticity. DS is the extremity of parasitic design. She is space and consumes the phallus in its naming of things, she exhausts the rhetoric of love in the abyss of simulation."

"DS stimulates Confessions?"

"I confess. The story destroyed me. It was the impossible solution to the narration of the cipher. As culture became analogical I wanted to be anodyne, speak a sopomorphic dream in the ear of eternity. I have destroyed the breath that inflated the model. I am breathless and will abandon you on the scene of seduction. I will start the story again. Wipe that smile off your face."

DS is a goddess. Hers is the universe of perverse volition. Her moods are manipulated by the DJ, recited with the masses into a moist memory. Everything is abandoned to the ruins of words whilst other languages seduce the senses. The power of words is their stake in other scenes. BPM is a matrix of oblivion. A speed ratio to describe rhythm.

DS works the rhythm to the bone and is submerged in other people's biophysics. Like Warhol she moves with the guiltless precision of a ghost. Only her image remains. Whatever the equation of her physical texture, her thoughts contain the seeds of her unique sensibility. She knows that the story is worthless. A cheap pornography in the Factory of Subjectivity.

I once imagined her reading Stentorphone in the toilets of Heaven. Dave had just invited Sally into his office. He was excited by the idea of interruption. A primal anxiety that manifests itself in public exhibitions of lust. Dave de Faray was a lecturer of English at Oxford. He was a born reactionary and lover of Larkin. Sally, a visiting lecturer from Sussex, found his ideas repulsive and feasted on his cock in masochistic delight. He dribbled semen into her ass and she laughed...

Å

"I c5t 4his sc`Ne out. No one reAds in clubs. OnLy wankers."

"So what happeNs next?"

"...Machinery of torture. Two lepers falling into the abyss of each other's wounds. This is the ratchet on which Stentorphone is master and often stretches DS to her limits."

The resolution of words is a mystery.

In the implosion that follows, some of those ideas have been decimated, abused in the rigor of life. Some prophetic interludes now seem trite but still the idea of her fetish for the text is interesting. DS wants to slip out of life into literature. This is a metaphor for our Western economy, the libidinal excess that binds fact and fiction in a smooth *fort da*, the oiled interface between us, the absence that is your presence, the breathless ambiguity of 'I love you'—*the flawed but felicific mantra of fuckers.*

DS and Julia leave Heaven together and catch a nightbus to Battersea.

Meanwhile, a carload of clubbers rolls on the way

back to Hackney. An ambulance arrives to the sound of Jolly Roger's *Acid Man*. A sardonic definition of tragedy on a speaker that dangles like a dismembered eye from the dashboard.

Every chapter is a decimal unit. Every paragraph a perverse universe. Nothing remains.

Nothing.

Between us.

Nothing.

There is fluff in the groove

Ú2 Chapter <2>
Ú2Ú ÚY Co d

Chapter <2>
Coda Cipher

destroyed the original. I stole the disk, a Maxell CF2. Mark looked everywhere for it. I steal all kinds of things but books are my favourite. The first book I stole was *Glas*. It was so expensive. I could buy half a gram of Charlie or pay a gas bill for the price of the elaborate economy between Genet and Hegel. I stole it from the ICA bookshop. When I got it home I found that it was all about stealing. This knowledge corrupted me and I worked through the bibliography. Books should be chained like old bibles to secure profit.

Real sensitives fuel my brutal appetite with more titles. They even write them on pieces of paper for me.

When Mark was out I would enter his files and abuse his writing, adding my own witticisms and references. I let Dolly Savage become DS.

I desensitised her. Stripped her of her crude naturalist persona. There were other writings on the files, stuff about Baudrillard and the economy of the sign, Kant and irony—serious Philosophical essays. I would pepper them with porn and androids. Mark seemed a little low on testosterone for a ladies' man.

When I moved to London I took his file with me. He didn't have a computer of his own. I also stole a couple of books. Just one or two titles had that seductive aura I collected; *The Madness of the Day, Paraesthesias, Gynesis, Diary of a Genius*, and *From A to B and Back Again*. Not an excessive amount of booty but Mark is scum. He's always skint and he's too stupid to steal.

After I moved he would telephone. He would ask how I was and I would ask if he'd bought a computer yet. Then on the occasion of one of these conversations he told me that he had given up writing and had become a living sculpture. He described the routine and it sounded like he had become a beggar.

Once I had stopped laughing I had an idea. I would finish his book and sell it. Serious journals published his critiques so with a little modernising DS could be an earner. If not it would be a laugh to send him a copy of a desktop print and pretend that I had got a publishing deal. If he freaked out and tried to sue me he would lose, because strictly speaking the story is mine not his. He couldn't secure legal aid to champion his rights to a novel about an inflatable doll. My *Come* was irradiant shards of the Philosopher's Stone. His was shit. In fact *Radio 4* would probably invite us on to discuss who was the original mystic mercenary, Mark 0 or Mark 1?

I would justify my position by serving them a slice from Cartouches,

> "*To take on anal excretion, swallow it or have it swallowed, to reckon on its enjoyment* (jouissance), *such was the rhythmic operation,*

the regular cadence of the 120 days. Each experimentation is meticulously noted, narrated, dated, and scrupulously accounted for. Arithmetic, compulsion and (ac)countable narration are part of the fun, they procure a supplement of jouissance *and leave writing no respite. Store must be set by excretion (oral or anal), it has to be taken into or onto oneself at the (secret) moment of its separation, and interiorized. But the introjection of the piece* (morceau), *in other words the bit* (mors), *is interminable, it always ends up letting drop an absolutely heterogeneous remainder of incorporation."*

I consume what I read.

He would come on all philosophical and I would act like a crim. When fact and fiction fuse, the effects are devastating. The media moves into position and *hey presto* faster than you can say, *Hel-za-pop-pin*, there are stiffs everywhere. I wrote the concluding chapter and typeset it.

In retrospect what transpired was slightly weird. Mark phones from Victoria and wants to drop in. Everything is uncanny when you're in. Home is the place where you lose yourself in all the telepathic networks of the future.

That's why people go out to work!

To get away from the uncanny calls.

I cleared the table and turned the computer off. I started cooking to put him off the scent. Chopping between garlic and subjects to talk about I realized how little I knew about other people's recipes. Unfortunately a pooka gangster I could only think of the ingredients that would incriminate me. I remembered a bit about Dolly on the train back from London. She was thinking over Seance's offer. The cinema promo for Stentorphone's novel. She had dozed off while reading at Clapham Junction. As she slept she had a dream. (You notice that even thinking about his arrival makes me call her Dolly.)

The book had grown fangs and had bitten her thigh. In her dream she was made of flesh and blood. This incision not only made her bleed but also aroused her. She wanted the fangs to stop teasing her and suck her love muscle. The fangs were after blood not vaginal fluids. DS was not alone in this fantasy. There was a man with a case watching her. The case was on his lap. An old case of beaten beige leather with frayed stitching. Below the silver clasp were two neatly stamped letters in blood red Times Gothic:

SF

I rubbed my fingers in basil to remove the smell of garlic. I threw the mixture into the oil. Why SF? I asked myself. Perhaps that was Mark's idea of marking a genus. Science fiction?

What was scientific about a vampire dream? Perhaps it was a metaphor for AIDS?

Her desire to become vulnerable to the viral intensity of desire?

I had erased a lot of the detail. The onion and garlic sizzled. I had a pang of regret. Was it guilt?

I remember I had stolen a first edition print of Bram Stoker's *Dracula* from a shop on Dukes Street in Brighton. When I showed it to Mark he told me that in mediaeval times rapists were put to death with a stake through the heart. His theory was that vampirism is a metaphor for rape. I always took him literally but perhaps he was being ironic.

Then maybe this was what marked the difference between us: I was more Thanatos than Eros.

All of this smalltalk is beside the point. I needed to distance myself from those memories of the book and focus on cooking. I opened a packet of spaghetti and put the pasta in the pot.

It was hopeless: I couldn't stop myself. I felt like a memory addict. I was seeing the cursor flash across his sentences, erasing the waffle. What was all that nonsense about the ass of the Hottentot woman on display in the Musée de l'Homme in Paris? A fine example of errant idiocy. Mark had written these scenes in which DS and her lover were walking through the Tate and talking about the politics of their relationship.

He was always rabbiting on about aesthetics, sexuality and the ethics of seduction. I always say, "Love is a fuck." Either Mark was lying or I had lost my sense of time. Before I had the chance to rinse the pasta he was at the door and giving the bell a familiar finger.

It seemed ages since we had been face to face. That strange mystery between two points held us apart. Mark and Mark. The invisible dagger manifesting itself, I opened the door and let him in. A pantomime of graces. He watched as I ate and talked about Voltaire.

After eating I offered him a coffee. He loved coffee more than Voltaire. We retired to the living room and talked until late. Then we watched some TV. A programme called *The Big E* came on and I started slagging off the people who had cashed in on the acid thing. Mark insinuated that I was a thug and my

Love is a Fuck

(25)

ideas were nostalgic. Nothing called acid house ever existed. The medium, according to Mark, is a viral hallucinogen in the psychotic spiral of information addiction.

It was pure Mark.

He was speaking that weird blend of words, part soliloquy, part somatic overdose.

I wanted to tell him that I had written the first novel based on the art of the remix. I wanted to tell him that he was a warm up, a piece of fluff to excite the crowd. Sacrifice the fuck on his own invention, let him chew his exquisite excrement, eat his way through my story of DS, the inflatable replacement for the late Dolly Savage.

It was an irresistible urge. I wanted to tell him about Anti Climax and the end of the novel.

But he sat there like a dumb fuck. Smiling, as if lazily emerging himself in the world's debris. Uninterested in his own thoughts, he continued to pump out sentence upon sentence of the un-edited masterpiece, the great morsel etc etc. I had heard it all before.

So I said, "Mark, you are talking bollocks. You have never had an idea worth stealing. Everything of yours is piss poor. Who wants piss poor ideas?"

Mark seemed amused by this and asked if that was what I really thought. I said it was.

Then he asked me if I had seen anything of Madonna.

I said I hadn't.

He told me that he had.

I asked him casually if he'd fucked her.

He laughed and said that they'd been having sex without secretions.

He asked me if I was jealous.

My mouth must have fallen off my face.

Mark reminded me of all the details I had erased. All the reasons I had moved to Notting Hill. This was all so profound. I was almost moved to confession.

Then I felt something close to evil formulate an appearance within me. I knew that if he was working on another version of *Come* he must be borrowing time on someone else's system. This meant that he would probably keep the disk on him, being of a paranoid disposition after the disappearance of his first novel. Leave the disk at home with all that derelict space waiting to become weird and consume important things?

I asked him if he had the disk. He looked suspiciously at me. A few cogs of intuition must have whizzed around to his Dept of Thought.

But I followed up with a rally of hysteria masked as fascination and made sure that the key didn't click. Mark was sucked in by his vanity and produced the disk.

My first idea was to make an accident happen. To destroy his new version. Curiosity overcame me. I also thought that he might even have a back-up copy. So I hit the E and entered the file. Mark sat beside me.

It was just like Mark had told it. Madonna was Madonna and the book was real. He had reconstructed it. Page upon page of alchemical equations fabricated in the tone of Leonardo.

Between observations on the Scorpion, the Bow, the Carthaginian War and the style of Pliny, he had written in the chance discovery of plastic. This was to be moulded into a human form and offered to his patron as an erotic gift with the message:

"Fame should be represented in the shape
of a bird, but with the whole figure covered
in tongues instead of feathers."

Notebooks 440 B 3 V.

I remember talking as I read, trying to sound
casual. I don't know if he was taken in. It doesn't
matter. What mattered was our Siamese texts. Then I
thought of the differences; theoretically we could
both get published. This I soon decided was too
romantic. The public like Gilbert and George.
Separation is complex. If I told him my crime he
would tell the world. Well, people he knows. Not
that he has a telephone book like mine. The literary
world is only a telephone call away. I see numbers.

On the screen was a translated text from the notebooks with a scanned copy of the original drawing.
The picture was titled *Incidence of Rays of Light.*

The tone of my voice must have been more sorbefacient than I had imagined. When I turned to ask
Mark who he thought would be interested in such a
story he was asleep. Of course I was interested in his
writing, I was a thief. Thieves always know the market value of things.

*Writers are scared of their depths and thus move
in the shallow zones of their texts.*

The reader is lacerated on exquisite oysters and
denied the pearls that adorn the ocean floor. Mark
was asleep again. His story was on the screen in front
of me:

Chapter 4. Scaffolds on Ice.

"What remains of the story?
Am I Stentorphone, the amplified
body of the deceased auteur
whose eyes secrete semen tears?
Did I dream this story of the
infant Leonardo?"
Her eyes closed. The book nestled
on her breast. Her dreams are my
theoretical stratagems. We flap
our wings to become dancers and
sink needles into her. The blood is
removed with somnambulistic
cool. We inject each other with
her virus. Death rushes into our
anaemic figures. Our veins dilate
to the size of scaffold tubes.
We arrive in a futuristic matrix. All
our destinies collapse and we
howl Piranha rhapsodies. Her
tongue swims on warm currents.
Her mouth is a red velvet cave.
She's kissing death. Death's
tongue is a silver train, twelve
couches long. Locophobics and
other passengers plunge towards
the climatic end but the tunnel is
an eternal metaphor. They emerge
in the whirlpool of black light... O

Thus the page opens multiple calligraphies surge to the surface. A bruised smile. Lipstick smudged over broken capillaries. Opium dreams and alchemical diagrams. The perverse cut that hauls all these stories together. A frivolous network of stray metaphors that spin around the needle, breathing, waiting, wanting knowledge. The infant Leonardo gurgles in the the dreams of Sigmund Freud.

I wanted to stop, rip open the seal and watch the cursor eat his words. The jaws of a labyrinthodon should entice his paragraphs to oblivion.

I thought of Leonardo sketching executions. Exiled from Florence he sat like an assassin training his eyes on their target. The face contorting, muscles in spasm, a mime drowned in details of the period costume. His hand guided by the knowledge of a mercenary in the era of Machiavelli. As a perspective materialised, I thought of murder.

Twice.

Murder has been called a passionate art form. This is because art evolved from magical hunting practices. The image fixes the object in the mind of the hunter. Mammoth or man, each is threatened by extinction as its coordinates are codified.

Mark slept with his shadow.

I pulled the disk from the computer and switched it off. I still had to decode how its existence affected our destinies. I looked at the disk. How different it is to a book. Where mythology and history were separated by marginal horizons the world is now a system of digital mnemonics.

Between zero and one a smile broke across my face. I was too busy to hustle the publishers. I would give my book to Mark and let him re-write his novel one last time.

I opened the box that held my disks and picked out one with a label of red insulating tape. I had picked up the habit of customising my disks from Mark. The standard CF2 was not a cool item.

Mark always used blue tape to mark his disks. I swapped the tape and deftly slipped his disk into my box and left the other on the table.

When he opened the file he would recognise the tone of my writing. He would know that I had switched the disks. He would also know that I was the one who had stolen his original version. If like me he had made a copy he would be able to laugh. Otherwise he would have to try and make me an offer that I couldn't refuse.

Pleased with my strategy I decided to celebrate.

I took a small wrap of coke from my wallet and lined up two neat lines on the table beside the disk. Unlike psychoanalysis, cocaine was a luxury I indulged in. Just this once I would share it with Mark. I knew he loved it although he could never afford a habit of his own.

"Oi. Want a bit of Charlie?" I said rather loudly.

He jumped like one of those torture victims whose senses have been destroyed by the political vigilance of its captors. His head jerked back and his eyes opened wide. I passed him a note and gurned.

"Very sexy crystals!" he said after sucking the line past the Queen's lips.

"Choo Choo," said I and cleared the line.

That night we finished off the wrap and bought a half gram that I persuaded Mark to pay for. We talke$ about the gram as an abstrabt particle of lan-fuage and the pervd2se traffhc be4ween idioms. Like newborn lovd2s our language was so in4ense that i4 seeme$ to repulse evd2yone who ,Ç<4>$@Ú¿?

The ethics of writing are like that of the firing squad.

His story is just a fantasy that bears no relationship to the surface vectors of life.

I have given Mark a game to play.

I have told him that Wilt found a dummy stabbed fifteen times and that plenty of publishers are giving good advances on fiction.

I was totally affirmative: what more can one desire?

LIFE IS NOT A FAIRYTALE.

Life is a sentence cut from a book and stuffed into a pocket. Like laundered money the bloodstains don't show and its context and origin become effaced by the perverse calculus of truth. Her suitors exit the page. Words are graves filled with exquisite letters that always know when it's feeding time.

Beware of sentences that call life to the edge for they are looking to end your elevated perspective.

Chapter <3>
Psychoscopia

Mark arrived at Brighton station at midnight. Still buzzing on the coke he headed for the Zap. He followed the route of a thousand day trippers. Down Queens Road, across by the Victoria and Albert Clock, down West Street and its arcades to the seafront. There he crossed the road and descended the stairs towards the beach where the club was. He arrived there to find a group of people waiting to get in. The club was small with a capacity of about 250. Mark used to work on the door so he didn't have to wait around. He was rustled past the group of leery lads trying to blag it.

Inside, the club was rammed with a coachload of Shoomers.

"All right matey?" said some geezer in a bandanna and blue dungarees, his face, neck and shoulders gleaming with sweat. He held out a bottle of poppers. Mark declined and moved into the dark cavern. Strobes and smoke created curtains of imminent light.

"You viced up Marky?" said Nick. Faking something close to drapetomania, that illness of sloth and wilful escapism legendary amongst black slaves, he moved on a pretty girl. Mark saw a few more familiar faces dancing but the majority were lodgers, showing Brighton how to party.

The bass thudded and the top end fragmented into wobbly Moog waves. Mark saw Anna through the smoke and moved towards her. People smiled and let him past.

Friendly fantasy without knots or riddles—no signs of violence or death except on TV.

Anna was a bit pissed and had brought two of her older students with her. The three Italians looked slightly dazed. English language books were full of pictures of Teds, Skins and Punks but this scene was a bit real.

Acid House had taken over where Rare Groove had met Mars. As Rock and Roll had been launched on post war affluence and Brillcreem, Acid House found its niche in the Wall Street crash and the surplus wad from digitalising the International Market. It was a wake for Thatcherism. A fusion of psychotropic soundscapes and a relapse into sixties-style hedonism. It wasn't in the tourist guides of '88 but it soon would be. Britain had long since stopped producing anything except hi-tech weapons systems and dodgy cults.

"Do you want a drink?" Mark shouted over the music.

"No thank you, Mark. I'm pissed already!" replied Anna.

"Are you on one?" asked Sean at the bar.

"Fuck off! Not tonight mate I'm with Charlie,"

replied Mark. "Sort us out a Lucozade!"

Mark returned to find that Anna had gone to the Ladies. The two students were trying to master the quirky movements that the other dancers were doing. Hands waving like tentacles in warm inky sounds. Like the other dancers they were smiling deliriously. Mark tranced out on the vice and didn't notice Anna return. She was laughing and pulled his ear towards her mouth.

"Is Boy George here?" she asked.

Before Mark had time to think whether or not it was likely, he walked past them looking wrecked and wearing the dressed-down kit of the other Shoomers. With this visual affirmation logged he replied, "Yeah. Look, see for yourself!"

"Is it him. Is it Boy George?"

An ethereal voice filled the room. The melody phased and panned around the club. Hands reached up high. "Reality, knowledge, feeling, truth. Reality, knowledge, feeling," then the voice sighed long and sensual and the rhythm kicked in. The dancers moved the current through a circuit. Zombies hiding from the cadaverous fears of the living, they let themselves become part of a network, a series of intensities that were contagious, seductive, deadly. They were the nightmare of E. Radioactive souls emitting pure equations.

"Mark, he fell into the toilet with me. I was sitting there and he fell in with me. And then guess what he said?" Anna asked earnestly, but she was obviously ready with the answer.

Mark raised an eyebrow and Anna filled in the space.

"'What do you think of orgasms?' He said, 'What do you think of orgasms?' And I said, 'I love them.'"

Anna was very excited.

By the end of the night everyone was dancing. The Faggot had moved seamlessly from *Phuture* into *The Promised Land* and everyone dripped with sweat as he worked two copies. With all the house lights up and the party still kicking it could have gone on forever. Eventually he span the record out and raised his hands in the air in a champion salute.

Mark made arrangements to meet Anna the next day to translate some sections of *Come* into Italian, and left the club.

Remarkably, Anna turned up on time. It was a sunny Saturday afternoon and Mark felt pretty good. The raptures of acid house hadn't damaged Anna either, although she did confess that she hadn't scored. Anna seemed relaxed and sat down while Mark got a printout of the voiceover for her.

She began reading from (sur)names.

Multiple frames roll. The vertical hold is going. Alternatively the screen splits open, smearing the canvas of Leonardo da Vinci with the excrement of Antonin Artaud. These two image makers, these serial effects of technology. In the background the television relays football from the World Cup. The film rushes like a train across Tokyo. The final edit is never realised...

When she awoke, the world was waiting to trap her in the embrace of desire.

The police say that Pasolini was beaten to death by a bit of rough. Before his death there is a rumour that Pasolini was working on the sex life of Leonardo da Vinci.

"Terminus Elle," she says aloud.

L —a letter snipped from the title of *LHOOQ*. The phonetic trace of the feline in French, surfaces as a unit in the economy of representation. Where other sciences repeat their experiments endlessly we are doomed by our own vanity to work in the dark. The words that surface here are the luminous traces of the deep-sea hunters. Psychoscopic explosions on the horizon of thought. Wild phosphorescence of an obsolete beast.

I situate us in the perfect theatre of her smile. We have no names, no faces, no story of our own. Clothes come off as the referee blows the final whistle. We fuck with the commentators discussing play.

Between the beautiful and the sublime is the scrambled text of Come.

What remains of the story?

Now as the horizontal hold fails my life begins. I am the mannequin and model upon whom this smile descends. I will tell you the story of *Come*. The indigestible morsel of the myth. This inflatable **L** for example. This mnemonic prop in the theatre of Philosophy. This *elle* that feeds the dream of the sleeping infant. The **L** that falls from the painting, tearing the canvas and revealing the hidden truth that sucks you into the whirlpool of words that bubble up from the breathing apparatus.

No really, that's enough, you get the picture. **L** is snipped from **L**over so you read 'over' but the subtitle loses the subtleties in translation. In my mother tongue she whispers, .

(39)

"Seduction is my destiny."

"What is this about?" asked Anna.

"Defacing Art," Mark replied enigmatically. Then, after pausing and looking at Anna he realised that she really was perplexed. Perhaps she was not into defacing Art. Italian Art was perhaps Holy to her.

"It's about tripping. Acid and its effects on perspective. You can buy trips on blotting paper impregnated with LSD. This is invisible to the naked eye but every trip has a tiny image on it, which helps you cut it up and consume a safe dose. The images are iconic: Gorbechev, Superman, *OHM*, Yin and Yang, Strawberries, all sorts. The other day at Spectrum I bought a tab with the Mona Lisa on it and it blew me away. The illicit complicity between drug culture and art, alchemy and reality all fusing in this tiny bit of paper. The icon became symbolic of the synthesis of art and science. Who made this thing and why is it seen as being a negative cultural artefact? In the Louvre the Mona Lisa is trapped behind glass. Tourists end up photographing themselves. In the sixties there were these badges that said, 'Support your local travel agent—Trip on LSD'."

Mark looked at Anna for a response. She had a weird distance in her eyes.

She laughed and looked at the floor.

"It sounds a bit crazy but I'll try and translate it." Her voice was full of bravado and she let a low laugh bark at the end of her sentence.

For an hour she sat and worked through the writing. Every so often she stopped and asked Mark about the context and conjugation of adjectives and tenses. It was difficult writing to translate. The irony of the scenario was that Mark knew no Italian and everything she said sounded wonderful to him. He loved her Lambretta accent. The way she revved her R's and reversed into the vowels. To him it sounded fantastic.

When she had translated it Mark set up the tape recorder and set the levels. Anna started to nervously shuffle the pages and scribble in corrections. She told him that it was her first time with such equipment. When everything was ready Mark rolled a spliff to chill her out and let her relax into the reading.

When she heard the results she was delighted but also slightly embarrassed. Her voice revealed something of herself that was invisible to others. Certainly Mark thought there was no need to be shy.

Fellini would have loved it.

Her voice had the lazy cool of the Mona Lisa. Rich and sensual, it had an internal drama that seemed separate from the words Mark had given her to translate.

(41)

It was a catacomb of whispers etched in iron.

When she had gone Mark listened to the tape again. A few sentences he recognised as his but mostly it seemed as though she had made him a gift. Even if his ideas made no sense to people, they would be able to relate to her voice. It drew you into a perspective and let you travel in its virtual dimensions. The voice, like the trace of writing, catches on invisible forests below the surface. Like a diver finding treasure that you've lost and returning it to you. The gift is a key to a place that has no name but myriad doors behind which your destiny recedes in mysterious steps.

A story that prepares us for death in the calm tone of a mother as she reads to her child.

Å

When Mark was six he fell into the sea and
nearly drowned. He went under the water
several times, screaming every time he
surfaced. He called to his mother who was on
the beach near the slipway. When he called
the salt water punctuated his sentence. It
was hardly a sentence. He was drowning, not
waving. His mother was pregnant with his
brother. To rescue him she risked a
miscarriage. She was furious with him. She
pulled him out of the water and dragged him
home. He was crying, saying nothing.
Watching the red dye of her dress running
down her legs, his mouth was filled with the
taste of salty burps.

Recalling the vulture descending on
Leonardo's cradle, this event was the
realisation of his own mortality. The
umbilical cord severed, he was afraid of the
strength of the current. The world was a
sublime system of shocks. Some pleasurable,
others terrible. Death focuses the point of
divergence between the two poles but with
Mark it also confused them. It released its
grip and he found the sublime pleasure of
the edge. The delight of falling into the
abyss, the wings of fate and the power of
love. If Freud was right and parapraxis is a
form of elliptical knowledge, a terrible
strategy that we hide from ourselves (as
addicts hide their addiction), this event
also marked him as a deadly shadow on the
horizon of the sixties, a flower child
swimming into the psychotropical future…

Academics have discovered that Freud's autobiography of Leonardo is a fantasy. Many of its founding details are located in errors. The vulture was probably a kite. The child's destiny is unenviable. The future never arrives, the code returns to its errors for pleasure. We are all passengers on a train of thought.

Home is not where the heart is but where time begins and the tunnel ends. Home is a memory that lights up inside; it draws you out of life into death. Where the Red Sea closed our history begins. We are Pharaohs from whom the prophet narrates a departure. Culture is a crashing wave that destroys the past and brings us closer to this ecstatic curve, this wave of love on which we surf. An infinite pleasure in a finite space, a collision of currents, metaphors, edits, body parts, geographies, trajectories…

BIOGRAPHIES ARE MEMORIES OF OTHER LIVES
NOT THIS UNIQUE EXPLOSION THAT DEFACES US
AND CREATES US

Not this rye and architectonic configuration, this voiding pleasure and catastrophe of articulation in the fluid dynamic of the text. Between the body and the wave we ride on a layer of synthetic foam.

Leonardo could have designed surfboards, as he spent hours watching waves and drawing their form. In his time, theories evolved from watching things closely. Looking curiously at things that others passed by.

Leonardo, like Mark, contaminated his speculations with ideas that he fished from popular books of his time. His notebooks abound with references that now seem antiquated and charming. The genius is a reflection without flaws. In truth we are flawed by the extremity of our nature. We are destroyed by the invention of new perspectives.

Moving beyond the looking glass we forget Lacan and the theatre of theory.

Between tragedy and farce I boast about your smile.

Freud was seduced by the idea of the Universal man. The Master of perspective and the definition of genius. Freud discovered that Lou Salome had more than a lush pussy. Together they consumed huge amounts of quality cocaine and wrote long lists of names for the sexual organs.

As we all know,

"There is fiction and there is fiction."

There is a nostalgia for the story that haunts Mark. He has a series of notes to help him reconstruct his deconstructed narrative. His smile is safe. Its placeless perfection seduces us as it travels between the Virgin on the Rocks, John the Baptist and the Mona Lisa. It is the banality of the gaze that is fascinating. Like dancers who become possessed by the beat, tourists gaze at the Mona Lisa. Beside her John the Baptist is alone. The masses are oblivious to the routes of their Culture. We are lost in the euphoric smile and its obscure chemistry.

Lost like Nietzsche in the web of his text, Salome (whose silky underwater so seduced Freud) calls for the head of John the Baptist. Her smile is the brilliant smile of forgetfulness, the joy of losing oneself in the addictions of others. She whispers to us in a language that is powerful and erotic. In blood she draws our attention to the trigonometry of power.

The web of blood and geometry collapses as our

story returns to the trace of the human cells—Mark. The debris of his over-fertile text.

In the daytime he would put on his hat and tails and pose for the tourists.

Standing absolutely still he became the antithesis to the frantic dancer. An aristocratic Buddha in a sea of phased pedestrians. They would throw coins that he could spend on drugs.

Unlike his story, his life was simple. Life existed between world-historic events. The cartography of being almost unscathed by the terror of a world that was quickly destroying itself.

His nihilism was somehow creative. Perhaps it was the ecstatic form of reality. A fatal stage that took pleasure in the horror that propelled him across the borders that would contain his biography.

Mark is a Christian name.

It is also a verb. It cuts this sentence off from its predecessors and lurks in the future. It becomes a territory. In claiming laws and conditions of life for itself, it risks war. It holds you tightly. Bound by the obligation of so many words. It risks untying itself from other trajectories to whet your appetite for more. It writes itself out of its will or place in the world to achieve power through pathological wounding and sacrifice. Waiting for Freud to say something. It castrates itself because it is also its inarticulate double.

Then it magically remembers itself and its labour of love, pulling a little harder on the thread that binds you. When I talk of Mark like this, I feel like Leonardo Da Vinci. He took pleasure in dissecting things and talking in the third person.

Between several marks and remarks are words that will burn through the hemp...

You

will

fall

into the flames

of

eternal temptation

in a

wet remix

of

Come

Chapter <4>
Disco 45

3ealots rock to the Todd Terry groove. The Ministry of Sound's custom built JBL system is pumping out repetitive beats. The Friday night crowd is going bonkers. The security are mincing about in their official jackets. Wide yellow smiles contort out of frame. Ecstasy enemas are delivered with complimentary tongue kung poo. Speed is licked from magazine wraps. Water is expensive and everyone wants it. Mark is one of the masses and craves its simple formula. The needle sits in the groove, a diamond tip tracing the spiral of information and passing it down the arm and into the mixing desk. Cryptic samples from film and TV, fragile bridges from reality. LA burns in video scratched symphonies.

It is a book that uses the impossible and anonymous star to fix the co-ordinates of an inexplicable sensibility

Older clubbers are thrown to the edge as the BPMs rise. Mark cruises the peripheries for eyefood.

IT is the autobiography of the era of mechanical reproduction. It is a superficial and depraved text that wallows in its vacuity and lack of psychological acuity. A cut and paste in yer face remix of Acidic grace.

DS is the illicit product of the sixties. Mark's father was Brian Jones. He fucked her mother on a flight to LA.

He died when Mark was five years old.

Narcissus drowned in his own reflection. He drowned to save us. Like Jesus he dives into the abyss and falls further and further from us. We are afraid of drowning in ourselves, of becoming a coherent image manipulated in digital systems. We have disappeared to become translucent. Anonymity is a surface to hide our knowledge. Clues drip like bloody honey on the page.

Where the fuck are you?

Speaking like this, in this affected tone of distance I feel your anxiety. There is no destination. The train is always late. The announcement articulate in the precise dialect of the other. No digressions, no semen, no incisions, or confessions.

Cocteau said of himself:

I am the lie that speaks the truth.

In his version of Orpheus a mirror is a pool and cinema a version of mythology. Poems are blank sheets of paper. Modernity is a world upside down.

The DJ has got a boxful of dodgy porno discs.

There is **No Destination**------------ ------------------------------

WE have a secret to share. A dimension of dialogue that is unique because it is ubiquitous in our world. Our world is dead. Mark and Mark have phased out. DS is in orbit. So what happens next is a secretive fix of COME. A deflowering of our virtuosity, the germinated seed of the underground.

The other book is called *Cum*.

It had a more obscure title once.

LSM.

Don't mourn over lost titles. The next one will always be more sensitive... (TULIP)... in tune with the code... (PARASITIC)... orgasmic on impact... (SEXY)... and virulently effective. This is the autobiography of an age. Inflatable moments into which we can transfer a little lust, life and love. This is the age of DS or artificial codes and layers of skin. This is the depth at which appearances become fatal and language is destroyed in the euphoric collision of vowels and saliva.

Hot plastic spurting over a cold metallic mould. In a future syntax (visionary horizon), I write my memories professionally, unloading all the details for the experts to examine. I will sell DS to the highest bidder. It is fuck fiction.

By the time I leave the Ministry I am wearing my Rubber Fuck Fantasy.

Words blank out the holes in our imagination and guide us in our orgasmic trajectory. I leave the club alone, my indifference to sex amplified by the quality drugs. Pornography suspends its economy until you want more and then you remember that every vice has a price.

Two beautiful girls ambush me on the steps of my flat.

"You got a light, geezer?"

I find a light before I find my keys.

I hold out the lighter and the black girl leans forward. She smiles and takes a drag on a reefer and blows the smoke at me. She smiles again. A psychopathic smile that is troubling and subversive.

The smile of a Black Planet or Solar Anus.

The white girl says, "I'm Cozy, want some?"

She opened her coat. My pupils expand at the rush of nubile flesh: she is naked except for a big pair of Caterpillar boots.

"What happened to your kit?"

"I swapped it for some drugs!" she says and pulls her hand out of her coat pocket to display a small plastic bag. Her flesh is creamy white and her pink pussy matches her needle-tipped breasts. A tasty scar just below her rib cage is weeping slightly.

"How did that happen?" I ask.

"Sfax and I were playing truth or dare."

"Can Cozy and I come inside?"

"Do..."

"Cozy likes to fuck strangers," says Sfax, closing the door behind her. Over her shoulder she has a black bag. She pulls out a camera.

"Do you want to star in a videofuck?" she asks casually.

"Are you serious?"

Cozy smiles and walks over to me. She takes hold of my belt and leads me towards my bed. She strips me. I open the wrap Mark and I had bought earlier.

"Can we?"

"Why not?" I reply.

She dips a wet finger into the coke and holds it out for Sfax. Sfax shakes her head. Cozy traces the wound with the powder. Climbing on top of me she lowers the wound to my mouth. I follow the crack in her flesh along the bitter trail of coke.

She then puts her finger in again and circles my throbbing cock with Freud's aphrodisiac.

She goes down on me sucking the drug like candles from a cake. Exquisite and silent choreography of sexual technique. I am out of my depth. Sfax hands Cozy a Durex. She pulls the rubber down my prick and terrifies me with her deft fingerwork and soaking pussy. It feels as if she's been fucking all night.

I'm stiff inside her. The succubine adoration of scars continues. This time I drop cocaine into the wound. This stings her. Her cunt clutches me. I lower my head to the wound in her flesh. A zig-zag signature below her left breast. Sfax has a vibrator.

My tongue searches for the coke that hasn't dissolved into her blood. Tiny crystals like boulders on the periphery of a volcano. Like the nasal cavity or the vaginal membrane, her wound provides the drug with routes into the blood system.

Cozy licks the wrap clean and drops it.

The vibrator; A dub sex machine with a secret history. A velocipede of transformative technology. The electric phallus is not a cock. Like the barrel of a gun it substitutes and defers the other tool in a transference matrix.

Unlike Cozy, Sfax remains straight and clothed. Her dress is a web of cream lace. Her nipples and shaven barbu, exquisite gifts of pornographic allure. Treasures adrift above her thigh-high boots. I fuck her friend; she practices her editing technique and direction skills.

"Come Mark, don't be shy, dish the cream!" she whispers.

Her face is partly obscured behind the camera. Shooting an overhead shot, flesh tracks, wet interludes.

"How many fucks have you got on tape?" I ask the camera.

Sfax smiles at me. It is a codified smile frozen in blood. The smile of the Mona Lisa, or Anti-Climax. A smile that is a rush of violence suppressed to realise a stratagem. I think of the Brazilian tapes, soft porn subtexts of personal politics, erotic molotovs that bypass the censorship of morality.

Cozy turns around on me, her buttocks dripping with molten entropic desire. Sfax jumps over the bed. A chocolate Alpine abyss of exposed vulva propelled on espresso thighs, scenic hallucination of Black Power, her lens draining the venery code that registered on my retina. My finger slides into Cozy.

She rubs my testicles in the entropic ooze, her fingertips threatening castration. I envisage razor blades and plastic dope bags.

I feel fucked. Stereoscopic soundscape of the phuture, bass and kickdrum, cropped blonde head moving to and fro. I place my hands around her waist and then raise them. *Her ribs feel like the stolen wings of steel dinosaurs.* She breathes like a monster from the prehistoric night. I have never had sex with a stranger before. This is a fantasy timed within the horizon of pre-viral sexuality. I see the golden durex disappear, a surgical perversion and realisation of infantile research. I am Mr Y and she is an insane victim of self-laceration. In her cunt I find the Tropic of Capricorn.

Sfax pans up like an insect. The prosthetic eye zooming in on the crimson vacuity of Cozy's mouth, white teeth and pastel pink tongue. Sfax has the vibrator in her hand. She moves around to my right and lets it buzz in my ear. An auditory diversion from her perverse proximity and distance.

I close my eyes and almost simultaneously feel the metal head against my lips. She parts my lips with the device and I don't resist. The machine is buzzing in my mouth. I am the centre of a cybererotic fusion of circuit-chic...

Å

I am the powerless star of Sfax's white skintrade epic, *White Boys Suck*. I open my eyes. I am sucking on the vibrator. Sfax winks at me. Cozy lifts herself off my cock. Turning around she takes the vibrator from my lips and runs it along the wound. My barrel is ready to unload into the Durex Gold. She takes hold of it and flexes it gently in her hand. With the other hand she runs the vibrator across my sperm sacs and slowly down towards my anus. It is someone else's story. She slowly eases it into the anus solar and then takes her throne upon my cock. The wound is raw and still seeping its translucent blood.

In mutual spasms of pleasure and pain we work quickly with pseudo-military efficiency towards orgasm. Sfax takes all the shots. A rapid succession of angles, spunky geometry of pubis and obsolete ruses of arousal. Pharmatropic propaganda for a perverse polysexuality.

Cozy gets up and her ass looks red. Her boots cool. Sfax follows her as if prowling a catwalk, a superfeline model of nihilistic fecundity. I was the ecstatic prop. *Infant penis sleeping on my stomach.* They walk across my room and Sfax follows Cozy out into the night in search of the next fifteen minute star.

I wish I had a camera or they'd invite me along.

I never saw them again and don't know why I told you so many lies about what really happened. The truth is sometimes more painful that fantasy. Fantasy codifies pain of living between the lines.

Soon *White Boyz Suck* will surface in women-only screenings where Sfax and Cozy will mutually masturbate each other as Sfax laughs at her macro technique.

ORGASM DESTROYS THE CONTINUITY OF TIME. SPACE BEGINS IN THE CREATIVE AROUSAL OF PERSPECTIVE.

Sex has nowhere to go but back to its origins. I never tell people about my sex life.

Short **term memory** loss.

Å

SEX DRIVE ERROR

Chapter <5>
Deep Dream Remix

> *"Where solitude endeth, there beginneth the market-place; and where the market-place beginneth, there beginneth also the noise of the great actors, and the buzzing of the poison flies."*
>
> XII FN *Thus Spoke Zarathustra*

Between a show on Tantric sex and a story that became incomprehensible, I found myself speculating on placement advertising in literature.

Was *American Pyscho* literature, or carnivorous sales talk?

Target marketing. Words, like products, must search out a niche in the market place.

Literature and cinema are attaching clamps to the erogenous zones. Lost in space, I watch as a machine tests a pink durex. There is a woman's voice. Then there is a woman. Like DS she speaks and I mediate, a mercenary in the field of information. Hers is the voice of experience. She hums pop songs to herself as she works. She operates the condom conveyer belt in a prophylactic factory.

The history of advertising has hardly begun. When I return to the institution I will have to dedicate my time to mapping out the evolution of AIDS imagery in *The Codification and Control of Deviant Eroticism*. It will be a mature work of reason. Politically correct and socially redundant, it will sit on the shelf in a lubricated sleeve. All the students will want to borrow it from the library. They will xerox the photographs and steal the fetishes.

The woman in the factory is busy because as we all know there is a boom in the market. The technology seems primitive: rows of metal phalluses perform stretch tests on the rubber. This economy is lubricated by tongues. The factory system, like sex, seems destined to become a nostalgic memory. Like science fiction, sex will change its name to stay hip. *Reading these seismic tremors arouses the production of nervous impulses.* The machine seems to have acquired the pornography of mechanical gestures. Commodity fetishism climaxes in the interface between humans.

Excrement and blood are kept in virtual shrines. Fluid interference between cells sends the needle off the scale.

Learning is the art of overcoming instincts.

The night before I saw an old guy on TV. I couldn't write or read so I watched. He spoke about early army-issue reusable condoms.

Geronimo looked perished, a penis discarded by Madame Tussaud. The old man handled the fluid trap like a holy relic. It was the only surviving evidence of his days of non-reproductive pleasure... DS is produced in a factory similar to the place where condoms are made. She is non-perishable and re-

usable. Her surface has evolved like that of the condom. The aesthetics of these items are like scar tissue.

They contain the body fluids and the discourse of
hygienics but aren't like flesh. Flesh participates in
sex. DS is troubled by this clinical aesthetic. It is true
that she is a model like other models, serial number
PZ092. She is a com-
modity packaged and
distributed according
to the market value of
the product. The box
she came in was like all
the others. Destined for
Japan via an ad in
Flash, she remembers
the cute picture of her
inflatable bimbo pro-
file, the bimbo text in
pastel pink symbols.

The TV is an
abstract arsenal of
moral codes.
Grandad and
Grandma aren't just
giving us friendly
advice. They are an
articulation of the
moral order that
lurks beneath the
frozen tip.

(59)

The value of the product had risen within her own
shelf-life. The economy of Japan was very faddish. In
the porn emporia some items became fetish icons.
After nipple clamps had come transparent dildos, pot
noodles and then... WOW!

Three price rises in a month. A whole lotta Yen.
DS was heading for the States, bought by a
Californian who collected erotic memorabilia. Inside
the packaging she was like any other doll. He could
have bought her in San Francisco for half the price.
But he liked the packaging. He was some New Age
Pervy King who knew how to impress his freaks.

He didn't keep her in the box of course. He used
her. He even customised her. DS was revamped to
look very hardcore. Fake scar business. That was
how she got her first film part.

A friend of the Pervy King used to rib him about how obsessed he was over his inflatable spunk trap. Then this other freak comes up with the idea of using her in a film he's doing with Dennis Hopper. Hopper was to play a fucked-up dealer with a psychotic fixation on this inflatable doll. The Pervy King was very jealous of DS because he loved Hopper.

Dolly got to be around Hopper quite a lot. The guy had an affinity for her. She was flattered. He would fuck her sometimes at parties, whisper to her between shoots. It was a dreamlike period in her being. The film went on to be a cult smash. Crispin Glover in particular ravished the lexicon of amphetamine babble.

DS was not nominated for an Oscar. But what the fuck. Neither was Hopper. He was fantastic. The most touching moment in the movie was when he stops the killer from molesting her and screams as he hugs her, "I ain't no fuckin Psycho—I *know* she's a doll!"

DS later described that celluloid moment as a spiritual climax. A peak from which she has had to descend with caution and grace.

She got another film role almost immediately and the Pervy King didn't stop her.

It was a lesbian thriller. A low budget arthouse movie. It was very politically correct and sensual in a dumb way. DS was only offered a bit part in a pornstore—a rather blunt flashback to her origins, but with none of the Japanese exoticism. She was just dragged out of a drawer in a New York store, soft and deflated.

DS understood that the film was a putdown of the whole male psyche, but this didn't make her feel good. The Pervy King didn't help! He didn't send her to therapy or even talk about her identity crisis.

He just fucked her like a dollar sock.

Unfortunately for DS the Pervy King had a friend who was developing a VR scenario. This began to shift the whole paradigm of the Pervy King's attitude to his faded starlet.

Truth is she ended up back in a drawer.

Julia Kristeva has written quite extensively on the horror of abjection. DS began to crave a place in someone's fantasies. And it is at this trajectory that our lines crossed. I was researching an illustrated history of sexual paraphernalia and had been given the Pervy King's address by some friends in Brighton. I got out to New York on a Hoover ticket and decided to check him out.

I spent a week there. Every day I would call around with my camera and shoot a couple of rolls of film, discuss the prints from the day before and record conversations with the Pervy King. His knowledge on the subject was truly encyclopaedic.

To cut a long and seedy story short, he gave Dolly Savage to me.

Then she was launched into the narrative of *Come.*

In this story her lover betrays her. The details are pretty dull. Tragically so. Her lover met someone at an ICA seminar on Cyberpunk. Dolly located her lover but she hadn't calculated on the video surveillance system.

DS was terminated with multiple wounds to her body. In the dead of night, two laughing women threw her into a bin. Silenced forever, in the morning she was thrown in with other plastics destined for recycling. With thousands of Volvic bottles her last cognizant moment was on a conveyor belt heading for reincarnation in her biopic.

L'ODEUR DE L.

1. EXT. BRIDGE, NIGHT.
A body floats into frame and under a bridge. It is an inflatable doll covered in body paint. In her mouth is a speaker. Her face fills the screen. The speaker emits an eerie recording of a woman's voice,
"You can't fuck with me."
The screen goes black.
Two letters L appear as the angles of a frame in which are seen, distorted 16mm footage of, a couple engaged in foreplay on a silver sofa. The frame breaks up and the words "Odeur de" *slide into the centre of the screen. Thus the full title appears in a flickering animation of text.*

2. INT. BEDSIT, NIGHT.
Starting on a macro shot of a keyboard, on which a man's fingers are typing in the letters, 'C-O-M-E'. *The camera pulls out to show* ANTI CLIMAX (or MAX) *at a table with an open book and a computer. He is translating an English text. The camera takes frantic close-ups of his face and then pauses, as if engaged in his thought processes.*
MAX: Merde! Au moins je pourrais lire ça et sachant que L'histoire s'est tenu. "Comment?" dit-elle. "*L'odeur de L*," replique-t-il.
The camera pans around to his ear and the image breaks up and is mixed with distorted black and

white images and animated sub-titles. In the disrupted frame we see a woman, SEX, on a leather couch wearing a set of seventies headphones. She is decoding the erotic particles of spectres that envelope her. Perhaps it is the voice of MAX in stereo.

—Écoutez, un parfum, l'odeur de la seduction au bord de la route. Des Philosophies du motel et du desert. Obsession. Une promotion du film noir tranche le psychisme, les jambes ecartés, lisent; Nausée, Nomenclature, Velocité et Collision.

3. EXT. BRIGHTON, SUMMER DAY.

A spinning air vent. MAX *walks past the spiral blades and is followed by a low scanning camera. He makes his way past the Grand Hotel, through the subway and onto Brighton beach. Amongst the old pillars of the West Pier he reads into a cassette recorder. With his fingers he gently spins the water in a rusted iron socket that used to support the original superstructure of the pier.*

MAX: Mais ça c'est pas L'histoire.

4. INT. BEDSIT, NIGHT.

MAX *(smiling as his voice fills the room)* Il faut rappeler que le faux a une verité que pendant qu'il reste fictif.

He leaves the cassette in the stereo and lets himself out of his room in the knowledge that the story will continue in his absence. We cut to SEX, who is again on the couch, wearing headphones and lying face down in a teeshirt displaying the message, 'Blow my Mind!' We see MAX *from her perspective as he watches her through a large glass window. In her headphones his voice...*

—Dans des livres, regardez-même dans les égouts! Nous disparaissons, pour revenir. Le plus que nous somme morts...

5. INT. LOUNGE, NIGHT.

From MAX's point of view we see SEX stretch and grab something from the concrete floor and hurl it towards him. It is a soft globe used by money traders to release stress. It impacts with a playful thump on the glass.

SEX: What do you want?

MAX: I've got some software for you.

SEX: Yeah, ok! I'll come when... I'm ready.

6. INT. BEDSIT, NIGHT.

MAX is in a silent orange room. He is busy laying out red material next to an orange and a plastic bag on a silver sofa. SEX enters and sits down in front of MAX. We see that her teeshirt has an inflatable doll's head on the front with a gun sight centred on it.

MAX: Shall I read to you?

SEX: No, don't bother, I'll listen to the tape.

As if this were a command, MAX picks up a walkman and a set of headphones and passes them to SEX who is winding on a throwaway camera. He stands slightly stiffly in front of her.

MAX: It's almost over between us?

SEX: Yes, I know.

Max: *(laughing)* The Death of the Author.

SEX: Are you ready?

MAX: Is the camera loaded?

SEX: It only has one life.

MAX: Oh, so what shall I do if we make a mistake?

SEX: Let me think about that. Tell me about the software?

MAX: It's on the system. A translation engine. I've become obsolete. You can play Chinese whispers with *Come* in any language you like.

SEX: Press play for me.

MAX *presses play as* SEX *ties him to the silver sofa. His voice fills her ears. She pauses between knots to photograph his bound body...*

—Désesperement, avec une éponge que j'ai emprunte, j'essaye de les éponger..

SEX *interupts her shots only to whisper inaudible things in his ear. Hitching up her skirt she climbs onto him.* MAX *smiles in complicity and raises his head to let her insert the orange into his mouth. Perhaps his cock is guided towards her barbu. Anyway his voice, on the cassette, continues....*

—C'est déja trop tard.

(65)

The screen breaks into fragmented black and white 16mm and Super 8.

SEX: *(narrating a voiceover)* The image develops in the field of vision, flirting with condensed narrative techniques of pornography. CUNT is opened to allow his COCK to sink into its warm galaxy. Sorbefacient fragments of promiscuous culture draw the voyeur into a gaze that is never returned. *L'odeur de L* signifies all that is submerged in the scent of LSM. COME is ejaculated as MAX allows himself to be destroyed in a low budget simulation of *In the Realm of the Senses.*

As her fingers bruise his windpipe and his eyes bulge, like Gilles de Rais, the voice of the narrator contin-

ues oblivious to the scenic transformation.

　　—Déja je me trouve dans le clôture doux de représentation. Des mots me lient dans un fantasme puérile de possession. Comme je gigote, ça devient de plus en plus difficile à faire.

Fade to black.

7 INT. BEDSIT, NIGHT (LATER).

Fade up from black. SEX looks out over the city. It is dark. MAX is motionless on the bed smiling like Leonardo's Bacchus after becoming the physical object of his patron's lust. Trapped in the black and white rushes of Brighton Rock, his memories of her spinning like Pinky's message, "What you want me to say is I love you but…", *eternally looped for cruelty's sake.*

Turning from the window SEX walks over to the stereo. She ejects the tape and walks over to his answer machine. She presses play and a series of messages are repeated.

　　—N'est-il pas du plus mauvais goût que la femme s'apprete à devenir savante… je l'imagine souvent versant des larmes sur son ventre… le monde vrai devient enfin un fable…

This is my vertigo of consequences as
sex becomes the contamination of
every scene with the seamless erosion
of its

meaning

sex

—becomes a sign for the break up of phantoms

—*is the ether of communication*

—focuses the scene as a transitory space

The cycle
of breathing,
eating and thinking
is terminated in the curious

gaze   **other**

of the

Chapter <6>
Necroticism

*"The text is a fetish Object
and this fetish desires me."*

R. Barthes

was so bored earlier, that I opened *Come*. I saw it for sale in Camden and nicked it. I had the money but why should I pay for my own tale? *Come* slipped inside my bag with purloined items by Dexter Wong and D&G. I moved across to the non-fiction shelves. I was searching for *The Lost Dimension*. The vertigo of the bookshelf overcame me and I headed back to the studio. After the burnout of editing I forgot my stash until now. After reading the first chapter I decide Mark has narked the plot and the narrative is out of sync. These are the seams that have inspired his readers. I pick up the phone and dial 01273... He is out. I wait for the tone and leave this message.

"I am telling you a story."

"I am a ventriloquist."

"A preacher of addiction."
"My act goes like this."
"It's a memory trick."
"You have lost the plot!"

Still pissed, I cut myself off. Where is he? I read the blurb again on the inside cover. Where is an acknowledgement of *Come*'s debt to me? He knows Jack Shit about ethics, for all his affected silence and unspeakable crimes. Wanting to numb out I switch on the TV, attaching myself to the abandoned terminus of the metropolis.

I channel hop. White noise pulsing between random scenes. Macro text reflected in the retina of hooded of stenographers, fluid pan from their quills to scribbled equations in the margins, stress calculations of the edifice... A moon casts a razor blue light across the victims... the sleek curvature of *Body Form*... the monster is chewing an eye. and e-mailing it to mark@marks.co.uk. A panoptic erection snorts the clouds from the sky. Only the brightest stars shine across the corpse.

A wave of letters orphaned from the previous film: DS... LSM... COME spell out the names of the stars in order of appearance. A list of credits that is endless and incalculable, a debtor's paradise. Doctor X begins at the end. The... that never arrives... but keeps you waiting wanting... for you to justify my... love... my

LOVE.

21

One starry night Mark falls asleep in front of the TV. In his dreams he pursues pure black only to be phased by the interference of continual colour. A voice in the bomb-torn room. Uttering its ambivalent desire like a renaissance masterpiece. Madonna on the rocks. Coke-can pipe with ash filter. Blacked tape, timecode, headwank, jet of of bile that melts lesser inflatables… end of transmission. Pure audio static after the tone.

Å

Dr X, or Stentorphone as he is sometimes called, caught a tube to the university. As he read the adverts he realised he had left his notes at home, in his handbag. He was a TV and often came to the University in drag but today he hadn't had time to do himself up. He had to give a lecture, BPM, *Beyond Postmodernism*. Beside an advert for safe sex he read a slo[+]mo advert for Dillons. It was pomo in a very 80's way. A simple reproduction of a dictionary.

(71)

> **nŏ´vel,** *n*. **1**. One of the tales in such a collection as Boccaccio's *Decameron*. **2**. Fictitious prose narrative of book length portraying characters & actions credibly representative of real life in continuous plot; **the ~**, this type of literature; hence ~E´SE, style characteristic of inferior novels. **3**. (Rom. law) new decree supplementary to the Codex.

> **po´etry,** *n*. Art, work, of the poet; elevated expression of elevated thought or feeling in metrical or rhythmical form; quality (in any thing) that calls for poetical expression; **prose ~**, prose having all the poetic qualities except metre.

"Yes," he said to himself. "I shall spin these two

definitions, crossfade some old and new tunes."

It was an affirmative Yes or Yea (it becomes Yo). Stentorphone's voice is on high metal heels, mixing a patois language to scratch the tympanum. There is a breath between thoughts, it propels and disrupts his journey. The other passengers watch him breathing whilst thinking about the parergon and the remainder (that which doesn't make the final remix). DS inhales the scenario, her body deflating between ideas, in empathy with his rhythm and the swaying tube.

Breaking from his thoughts he noticed a Guardian headline, *Second Chance for Bluebeard*. He read as a pilot reads the navigation equipment in a fighter, the object on the screen a simulation of a real object, a dotted matrix of lights in a formal harmony. The print was very tasteful. Below it was a line drawing of the French warlord, Gilles de Rais, looking a little like Marlon Brando.

Dr X entered the lecture theatre like an assassin. Obsessed with the termination of his subjects.

"Hello," he said, warning them, "I am mourning under the slightly heady epitaph, *BPM*. There will be no preamble to this lecture because I have forgotten my notes, however the tonality of my address should become miraculously clear."

As the familiar drone of a lecture began, the theatre lights were lowered and various students slouched forward onto their notebooks.

"I want to start by quoting Avital Ronell, 'We have to cut this shit!... Drugs it turns out, are not so much about seeking an exterior, transcendental dimension—a fourth or fifth dimension—rather they explore fractal interiorities.' In an early essay *Force and Signification*, Derrida quotes a famous maxim,

'To dance with the pen one must first learn to dance with one's feet.'

"The gramophone disc has a double margin. The outer margin allows the user to cue its accoustic trace. The interior spiral is more obscure, sometimes it is a locked groove, or a wax tablet on which machine operators have inscribed some cryptic code. For example, 'Robots on Safari.'

"Since Edison's invention of the phonograph in 1877, the stylus has traced the tracks of the groove. Edison's hearing had been impaired by scarlet fever, and when railroad co-workers playfully lifted him by his ears onto a train, his condition worsened. Thus, might we imagine that the inscription of the stylus replays and amplifies his delirious pursuit of sound along the railtrack of his unconsciousness? To the Victorian parlour Edison's speaking phonograph introduced a mystic transportation. It began with, *Mary Had a Little Lamb* and continues beyond Baudrillard's observation that now, 'We are vacuum packed like records.'

"Every groove is becoming a rut. The velocity of the mix sinks this information between the Western hemisphere under the sub-heading of *Kant,* or *Delirious Poetics,* and the Eastern hemisphere under the sub-headings *Spurs, Clubs of Rhetoric* and *the Demonic Jest of the Crypto-Amnesiac.*

"Dancers destroy the pessimism of the margins and engage with the scenic depth of *Pure War.* A war between rhythms. *BPM* is a philosophy, for the, 'Perhaps' generation. A "Syat" that fuses all the, buzz without the fuzz. Cool... just change the script and keep me on line for the apocalyptic sub bass. I am the amplified voice beyond occult symmetry. My spur is a submerged totem ejaculating into the grooves of taboo.

"Drifting through underground tracks, theory departs from familiar stations, there is in my voice, a debt to truth. Thus I remind you,

'There's actually no such thing as jungle.'"

Like Plato a few students are wearing personal stereos for protection and bugg out to, *Bogus dope Eschatology*. Between speed and politics others like Simone and Sadie sync up Stentorphone to, *Gulf Gansta*. The bass and sly snatches of familiar tunes disarming the listener to the collateral damage;

Ain't really a life.
Ain't really nothing but a drive by.
Desert stormin'
The jungle tonight.
Aint breakin' the law,
Just keepin' the score,
Ain't really a life
Ain't really nothing but a movie
Aint really so bad
The weapons we had,
Lit up Bagdad
Or was it Compton on the 4th of july?
Ain't really a war
Jist N.W.O. promo tour
Like Nike says, 'just do it.'
Gotta survive,
Ain't really no death
Ain't really nothing but a movie.

Over the backing track, Stentorphone continues,

"'Drop it,' says Derrida.

"'You have 30 seconds to comply,' hiss the other hashishins.

"Philosophy now is the amplified rap of street credible hustlers. Players on the ideas market. Drugs effect the human machine. Every pleasure is a code exhausted as we are drawn to obscure stakes. The stake is a magnetic needle spinning in all directions. The remix vampirised the original and deceives the broken memory. The needle spins a web of traces, rushing peripheral rhythms through the medium. We are mirror stage visionaries lost on the dancefloor. We are pagan telepathies, *BPM*, waiting for necrophiliacs to toy with the remains of our multiple tracks.

"I have forgotten my lipstick. But read my lips.

DON'T
DON'T
DON'T
DON'T
DON'T BELIEVE THE HYPE.

Å

This is supplementary to the Codex. The dub mix has less vocals. Stentorphone drops paragraphs that really move air. Deep noises from a dimension of elliptical thinking. Repetitions of an implosive moment, a sampling technology focuses on the literature of the Big Bang...

An echo in space.

1.01. What is literary about Literature?

DS reads Stentorphone, inhaling each scenario, her body deflating slightly in the lull between ideas. She speculates on her addictions. Her love for novels. Her ability to fold her pages in an anachronistic fashion and believe in herself as any other body without organs might do.

She speaks to herself but the reader sees quotation marks, hypertext links to other parts of the book that don't employ her as a voice.

"Which one of the Marks wanted me to be a dream doll or voodoo thing? This essential female, melted down into a crass receptacle for misunderstanding, a difference generator. Enough of being a narrative trigger. I want more air!"

Å

The sky is a piece of blotting paper with ink spilling through it, staining it, as in Hardy's *Tess*. Or is it the pharmakon that flows into the story through the process of printing? The letters SF are illuminated signs of another discourse. Let your eyes breathe in the romance of perspective. The red lips of Tess swallowing the strawberry. Imagine the unmapped territory of her oesophagus.

"The biodynamics of her consumption are like mine. Her interior is full of fecundity, trapped and decomposing like a serial killer's shrine. My story begins normally enough.

"Once upon a time there was a factory—it produced inflatable dolls. These were produced to suit every taste; from *Baywatch* inflatables like Tara, with her suntan, 'sensitive mouth and inviting vagina', for merely £30.00 to Cleopatra, whose price of £569.75 was

Let your eyes breathe in the romance of perspective. The red lips of Tess swallowing the strawberry. Imagine the unmapped territory of her oesophagus.

due to her extensive list of features including 'movable limbs, real human hair, battery powered vibrating-vagina, firm breasts that lactate, juice gland' (for when she gets overexcited) and 'a plethora of special effects that define excitation, for the sophisticated user'. These stories have a unified tone. They employ the devices of alliteration, rhyme and repetition. A story of this type often begins with the absence of a member of a family. An example might be the six wives of Bluebeard. The seventh wife is compelled by her curiosity to discover her destiny.

"I stretch in an effort to free myself of these zones, to swap sex drive for narrative drive. But my story drifts beyond the plot. Like sex it is subject to inflation."

There is always a difference between a plot and a story.

There is always a difference between a plot and a story

£

"My plot unfolds in a narrative. My story is told according to the apparent parameters of Real Life with due attention to cause and effect. I am the first narrator inflater. The plot is the derailment of these sequences, my flickering persona and sense of flashback. Language, like space itself, is a spiral of infinite relativity. A delicate web of digits that can be read like codes—repetitious statistics. The space stations of semiotics are crowded with philosophical junk.

"I was made in Hong Kong. My original name was Eko…"

The text is never what it seems, its seams are loaded with puns and punctures.

Unfilmable like death.

Language for Freud was like the Unconscious. It

surfaces oddly, in uncanny slips of the tongue, in theft and displacement, in a libidinous exchange between the economies of Eros and Thanatos: the two monster constellations in the Human Galaxy. I drop Freud and hurtle into the future that seems never to arrive.

Language for Freud was like the Unconscious

Marshal McLuhan said that billboards would replace the classrooom. He also claimed that electronic writing would replace the ancient hieroglyphics of calligraphic cultures. *The facts are fractions of an electronic simulation of space.* In these digital shadows the story of language travels unchecked by the border guards who would like to charge you entry into this bright new phantasmagoria.

Edison destroyed the cult of the Sun. The story travels beyond the speed of light to keep up with its reader. Information is measured by the speed and accuracy with which it is transferred from one space to another. How perfectly the code can be replicated.

The detail is fractal; words, like transistors, become micro chips. People become automata or demonic jesters. 'To become a star, one has to be down with the jargon of ironic redemption.' Dennis Hopper told me that.

In these digital shadows the story of language travels unchecked by the border guards who would like to charge you entry into this bright new phantasmagoria

Å

I should be read as the cartographic tremors of a despairing aesthetic. The model of receptive subjectivity on whom to recline whilst contemplating the virtual boudoir and…(+)… HIV Philosophies… The manifesto menu reads: Destroy the ideas market with ghosts from the catacombs of Paris, cuntish questions, gynetic aphorisms and clutter a space that is emptying itself for business. (DS, *folio.94*)

Å

Mark wakes up to the assaulting tone of breakfast TV. Has he been dreaming these voices? From within the confines of a brightly coloured fake living room, the chat-show hosts recoil in horror. Colin Wilson is waxing lyrical about the 'Dracula meets the Bride of Frankenstein' dynamic of Fred and Rosemary West's relationship. The hosts don't know how to end the interview or respond to his light-hearted resumé of their blood orgy. They must have heaped the coke onto the cereal. Something is very wrong indeed. The mood shifts abruptly as they announce the next item, following the death of another teenager on E.

(79)

Semiotics is a software package for Literature.

TV is fucked

New York is fucked.

Tokyo is fucked.

London is fucked.

The Capitals are fucked.

Art space is buzzing about

*"If you really believe in nothing
you can write a book about it"*
183
The Philosophy of Andy Warhol.

PORNOGRAPHY AND PHILOSOPHY
ARE PRISONERS OF A SPECTACULAR JOKE

Æ

.DIY.

PHOTO MONTAGE

WHIP

Ú3 IN Ú3

Ú Chapter <7>

Chapter <7>
Vogue

he story is all around us. Through the cathode ray womb it whispers like a promotional futures market. It is a luxuriant remix of *Come*. On the dancefloors, everything is normal. Sex and Death accelerate the body to the wavelength of the DJ. On necromantic ether he drives the masses into a frenzy.

Anti Climax has returned to Paris with out-takes from the two duplicate narratives of *Come* and *LSM*. DS has been translated into French. In the catacombs they are reading her at COOL Stock Exchanges. The city of the drifters has become the centre of a cyclonic dubbing industry. The text is authenticated—given the white label. It becomes, *fort da*, the seminal trace of the underground vibe. Forget flashbacks—here is a deep genealogical tracing in the mycological groove. The needle hits the dopest track like a spur in the groin of the Trojan horse. The record is a rhizomatic system of samples.

In a building used by Henry Miller the transcription of the text begins in earnest in October 1997.

Previous versions are melted down into byte sized chunks. The fuck cosmologies become quickly stylised into religious waves of ecstatic voices.

Zero and one.

So already the rhythm is changing, and only my knowledge, (lost in the spiral groove of *LSM*) prepares me for the music of DS.

DS is an amplification of a signal, a fetish submerged in the everyday. Transparent stimulant, her voice is sexual. She is an actress. Her sexuality moulds itself to your desires. She turns you on and silently inflates the impotency of the model. Lines discontinued, empty houses, cars with radios stolen, these are the ruins that delight her, vague spaces where she can let you play with her. She imagines herself as Divine, scolding you for limping on her dress—a sequinned trace of damaged fabric leads us forward. With phantoms screeching in the daylight the memory hits me. Anti Climax is spent.

Zero & One

DS. Not even a proper name, not even a doll, a snubnosed noise of addictive dissemination. She is a flipside, a B-side, an international code of corruption, statistical matrix of Erotic Politics. X point of our difference. The story is soaked in whooshing and orgasmic bass. Blood carries HIV. It also carries MDMA. Death is a magical velocity.

Tomorrow, the taste for control… the story… proper characters… sequence of events… new beats… final mixdown.

He is called Mark, but is rather a multiplicity of voices. The book he has written, *A Short History of the Inflatable Doll*, is for sale in WH Smiths. It was

not the original. It was a smudged reprint. The prophylactic trajectory of the fictive inflatable. There is
not a real life story. I am a sign of the times pushing
circuit chic... I hear all the 'TRUE STORIES'.

In exotic salons black scorpions are used to stop
models getting erections. While Dali and Buñuel tran-
scribe cosmological biographies, the insects crawl
over the naked feet of the model. The model attempts
the poisonous pose of the scorpion. Cocteau is on
opium. In a reverie his friend Apollinaire is telling the
story of how Picabia stole the Mona Lisa. The finger-
prints were everywhere.

In an untitled essay by Barthes, Mark found the
bacteria for a series of stories about Leonardo Da
Vinci.

The first I have told you before, although not like
this. Leonardo invents an erotic automata for a
wealthy patron—a beautiful model called Mona. Her
sexual organs were particularly well crafted and devi-
ated from the line drawings on which Freud based his
infamous repulsion theory.

Another was the Da Vinci necrophile file—page
upon page of notes and translations from Latin into
Italian on the court case of Gilles de Rais. Leonardo
had become obsessed after finding a signature in the
front of a richly bound copy of *Metamorphosis*,
received in payment for a brothel design in 1497.

The third was a text on the strategic effect of bio-
chemical experiments by Leonardo during his com-
mission as a military technician. Barely recognisable
atomic patterns, developed by Leonardo from the
Black Death virus, hide a horrific tale.

Barthes had invoked the irrefutable facts only to
distort them, seduce the imagination with a mirror,
reflecting lines laid for perspective junkies.

*Le0nard0
da V1nc1*

Mark tries to hide these narrative crystals but as her plastic begins to age, DS is caught at bad angles. Naked, her nipples are semi-erased. Gratuitous erogenous fixation is wearing her down. Mark's writing is interminable; she waits for it to stop, breathe, vacillate momentarily so that a word or two of her own can be heard, but it is useless. It is as if she is being teased with a dream of becoming articulate. In the intimate spaces marked by the absence of Marks, her words search like lips in the dark... for someone to seduce. The story is just another trap. The stasis implodes us. The DJ is hot.

So the story goes... between them no one wrote it down or recorded anything. It wasn't done. It was all fucked out, the past, books, records, TV, ecologically compromised artefacts. Only paranoids record things.

The other reader deconstructs the story, deciphers the plots, DS, *Come*, LSM. The cipher reads the congealed gibberings, theorems on tonal shifting gear, hacking scams and sophist rants on turbulence and surface tension.

BPM rising. Live samples give the mix a raw edge. The sound is roughed-up to avoid sounding like pop. The ecstatic flow is easy to follow. The war just happened, a bubble burst, it was totally slack, a bedtime story, remember Vietnam. The drugs, the diaries, the tonnage of explosives. Sex is transformed by death.

LA burns and the sound of *The Super Sharp Shooter* is obsolete. Other tunes are being mixed down for the long summer rush. The world waits. Carpets lie torn in the windless sun of the infinite summer. Limbs dance to a frozen breakbeat and the road from Basra looks like an iced promo for Pompeii. Someone let the mood fuck up real bad.

DS is in the house.
Freaky dancer.
Drug head.
Dreamer.
TV guest.

Animated like an Arabian Knight, her particles drift in nomadic trails across an illusory horizon. She is a mirage of masked desire dismembered for articulating without compromise a different chronological perspective. She partied on the high vibe while governments supplied arms designed by psychopathic technophiles. It's cool. A time for dreaming. Between the *CJA* and MDMA, life is an equation in ruins, a culture of the artefactual debris of History. Time is the soapy abyss through which her body is floated. *Cum* is erased from her mouth. She speaks a clean language of cunt/cock aphrodisiacs, a mind fucking nutrient that dissolves with acidic appetite the story and its cartography.

Dump the data.
Load the War Machine.
Pump up the Volume.
Destroy the Mass.

Inflate your spirit and rise similitudinous sunflowers into napalm suns.

Inhale and suck the fuck phantom of the imagination from between us. Bark hideous poems from the coma to the Capital.

Death is a dying Art.

Sfax and Cozy add voice-overs and leftover dub vibes. The tapes are sold to hip magazines and decadent emporia of PVC sleaze. Destiny is realised in virtual sexuality, hard disk scenarios programmed...

pure digital data

Transmutative genes are trapped in the soft envelope of the prototype. Cozy and Stax modified DS with crude sensor pads. Engulfed in her, they began to play in the dimension of their body space. Tripping and colliding, their bodies merge in sensory pleasures. Mutually accommodating electrical storms, they feed each other's electro-erotic impulses to the max. In the phallo-vaginal orgasma of simulation, their tongues twist like obsolete wiring diagrams. Viewpoints phase in and out of focus.

Only the audio signal remained constant and this changed when Cozy customised the system. The Metropolis beyond the room is a distant field of reference—the dull location of the electro-junky. In an orgy of apocalyptic design, they saw the video of their transgenital meltdown. From a blurred interface the sound of double breathing signifies the proximity of the virtual orgasm. There is a mystical aura around the developing machinery of virtual reality. Like French-letters the texts ooze with promiscuous stealth and impact user-friendly come-ons. We are bound as Blake porches to the infinite chains of the imagination.

Sex is a virtual lay-line to the unconscious. A dreamlike tongue or digital dildo caresses the parts real flesh contaminates. An angel, you imagine the Other as an imminent violence, the masked voice a prosthetic distortion of your God. This reading is less scientific and involves fractal solomising of the Black hole. A positive negativity that is a coil screw.

ZERO/ONE.

Transmutative genes are trapped in the soft envelope of the prototype. Cozy and Sfax modified DS with crude sensor pads. Engulfed in her, they began to play in the dimension of their body space. Tripping and colliding, their bodies merge in sensory pleasures. Mutually accommodating electrical storms, they feed each other's electro-erotic impulses to the max. In the phallovaginagoria of simulation, their tongues twist like obsolete whirling diagrams. Viewpoints phase in and out of focus.

Only the audio signal remained constant and this changed when Cozy customised the system. The Metropolis beyond the room is a distant field of reference—the dull location of the electrojunky. In an orgy of apocalyptic design, they saw the video of their transgenital meltdown. From a blurred interface the sound of double breathing signifies the proximity of the virtual orgasm. There is a mystical aura around the developing machinery of virtual reality. Like French-letters the texts ooze with promiscuous stealth and impact user-friendly come-on's. We are bound as Blake poeticises to the infinite chains of the imagination.

Sex is a virtual lay-line to the unconscious. A dreamlike tongue or digital dildo caresses the parts real flesh contaminates. An angel, you imagine the Other as an imminent violence, the masked voice a prosthetic distortion of your GOd. This reading is less scientific and involves fractal sodomising of the Black hole. A positive negativity that is a cool screw.

a strict numerical dimension
or panoptical dream

The tech is not cheap. Neophytes must invest heavily if they are to become bodies without organs. Like VCR, CD and TV, DS is transformed by the technical vectors that encodes her. Cozy had found her on a shelf with Zara and Adam. Perhaps DS was trying to get some more info on UK models. Adam was modelled on Jeff Stryker. He reclined on his ankles to display his stiff sixty degrees. He was handled by both sexes. A Libertine adept she is used like a toy to navigate playtime in the syntax of power, sex and the other commodities that Sfax and Cozy thrive on. She is a partner in a digital threesome. She becomes expert in the laws of differed pleasures.

LSM was a format that allowed the user to flirt beyond the matrix. Cozy and Sfax saw her as a war machine in the zone of gendertainment. In classical terms her territory is marked by the deflation of names into nouns. Her name marks the boundary between the Marks, insofar as she spills the seed of their plot to infiltrate fiction with simulated subjects. For one she was the Other incarnate. For the other she was just a cipher for the invisible masses.

Howl your prequels to the sequential bass...bass...

H o l y — i s   t h e   a g o n y
Holy—the serial lover
Holy—the repetitious buds of Spring
Holy—the daisy and genital hair of adolescence

ВЯЯ offers a deflated commodity at an inflated price. Beyond the ZERO/ONE interface DS becomes familiar with the figurative gestures of the feminine. Sfax and Cozy are oblivious to her fascination with the minute detail of their lives. As they work during the day; phoning distributors, art house cinemas, printers, festivals, and engaging with all the tedium that is the flipside to their lucrative video-fuck business, they are scanned by her receptors. From her invisible position she would steal their easy sense of themselves.

DS wants more than real hair—she needs an authentic aura.

The visual resolution is not perfect, but better than a 70's pornflick. Erotic energy is efficient energy.

Soft responsive technologies are the future contour of smart environments.

Howl your sequels to the sequential bass...bass...

H o l y — i s   t h e   e c s t a s y
Holy—the serial killer
Holy—the repetitious snow of winter
Holy—the rose and sick worm of experience

---------------->>>>> *EXIST.*

*S*cientific researchers logged onto *Black Ice* for months. The Matmos threatened to involute them. The corporation's sponsorship of the dimension forces the masses to consume a fantastic machinery of representation.

This artifice of address—this **L** of simulation, spoken by this angel in the interior of the TV. A voice that mediates like the voice of Mona Lisa. A voice strangely silent as this phoneme animates my absence of irony.

"Already I have said too much and not enough. The adverts stage the implosion of our dreams."

Outside there is the darkness of the City. A phone rings.

"Hello, I'm interested in the way you translated the story."

"I remember frames, digits, narratives, we have spoken before."

"Yes, yes. You were telling me the story."

"Childlike voices, hallucinatory stench of war."

"You said that all Literature is pigshit."

"Did I?"

I imagine a smile. It is faint, as if you were practising. Then radiant, it breaks across your lips. Your teeth, like frames of film, glint in the artificial light of Tokyo at dawn. The future collapses in the impossibility of a beat between zero and one.

It's a wind-up. The ciphers are back. The wave is extending. The curve of the smile is rolling between frames. The superimposed negative is a dense tube.

Mark is standing beside a tomb on which is laid a Xerox of the Mona Lisa. It is a Super-8 movie. No dialogue. Mark places flowers on the smiling face. The surfer wipes out. The smile is both beautiful and sublime.

But only from certain angles.

The flowers are kitsch.

The angel is **L**.

The body in the letters of a literature of flawed flows. The hysteric that reframes the flowers by dropping them out of the frame. Leaving a signature without a date, a calligraphic density to be restored by experts. In a language like English I move outside of the frame and up the price of the dialogue. The aesthetic is drifting with me contaminating space with viral integrity. I speak but signatures slide from my lips down the line towards the seminal space of reception. My voice is cloaked in the digital, and its tense tonality sounds futuristic, a B-movie effect that puts you off the content.

Once I drifted into chit-chat, love, cars, books, but now... breathless and ill at ease, I wait without flowers and imagine that this sense of deja-vu is deceptive and that this exchange is original. Not a nausea, but visionary sickness.

"The interminable analysis of vomit, of a nausea rather, by which I am infected and which causes me to write myself," you said or someone said and through repetition you amplified that ambivalent sign. Illness and its metaphors.

have destroyed this limping paralysis, this wake without drugs. I have brought the desert here and mantras that fuel a breathing pattern to facilitate euphoric vomiting. Empty the system of digestion and allow the body the rapture of hunger. To destroy the voice of inner spirituality it is necessary to analyse an ocean of vomit.

"LHOOQ. Enough. It's over, drop it."

The voice signifies the proximity of trauma, castration in the pre-Oedipal trajectory of Art. **L** is the fragment of the name,

LEONARDO DA VINCI.

This other voice that comments from beyond the frame in the tone of the GREAT COMMENTATOR. Is this also vomit rotting the Ls that are bound in its constellation. It tries to hide the score and the stake of its claim to Universal genius. It speaks through several screens, idioms, systems, languages with multiple traits. It swoops returning the story to its origin. The breast recedes and the bird flies in. I sign for the flight. The name I enter is a pseudonym spelt like Leonardo da Vinci.

The false identity circulates according to the rules of Capital, becoming fetishised and thus accumulating value.

$$\text{ÚW} = \text{LSM2} \ (\text{VR}—\text{E} = \text{MC}^2) = 01\ 92\ 35$$

Ω will not dance tonight. The DJ is soft. Instead she conjures herself from *Gynesis*, "'There is no question of a woman here, but a metaphor' (*Disseminations*, p242) designating that which dances across the secure territories of truth, unsettling them. Ultimately, the metaphysical V of the dialectical *versus* explodes into the Derridean wings (*ailes* [L's]) of butterflies, the *angels* (L's) of the text:... leaving behind the *elles*, shes of a now (eternally) feminine writing."

The immaculate carnage of representation.

Ω loops inside its coiled *jouissance* and unbinds the simple historical trajectory between A and B. *We read texts to lace the narrative with fragments of the Pharmakon.* Already the double mimes these 'TRUTHS' and erases the name DS.

The paint is peeled away with sub-atomic precision and the perversity of the line is revealed. Its author a master of the Priory of Sion, spent hours hiding ciphers on the palms of her hands. She holds the key to the Temple of Solomon. John the Baptist is merely the guide.

> The paint is peeled
> away with sub-
> atomic precision
> and the perversity
> of the line is...

Q might signify that part which Dada destroyed. The active nihilism of becoming Dada overthrew the generic possession of the name. R Mutt, like DS, is an effect of the laughter that orbits the dead relic in which belief has departed. A literature of abjection, unheard and unsounded voices that cannot claim the value of a signature. The (invoice) debt circulates within the double chiastic invagination of her *envois*.

Something is sent, (especially in the senses of the message, missive or dispatch), the transitive sense of *s'envoyer* has a special slang sense in French. 'To send oneself someone' in this sense means to provide oneself with someone for sexual purposes. What can or cannot be translated, sent from one language to the next? What remains?

By these means, DS constructs from deconstructed fragments an ideal manifesto. The fragments testify to the ambivalent and violent act of seduction.

"She croons like a crane on her inflatable heels."

"Seduction is my destiny, seduction terminus **L**."

She is dubbed into Italian.

Do you remember these details, this mysterious detail of sceneless stories, sugary soundscape and proliferation of Zeros?

An 'O' opens in the centre of space. It is a ring and orifice of the solar anus.

The ZERO is infinite.

Twice. It is repeated in the name 'Leonardo'.

Flying around like cogs of subliminal desire, a War Machine of erotic trajectories shoots its load over the cradle of the sleeping infant. The bubble gum virus perverts the child and Pussy Galore comes with 007.

Virtuality is gadgetry for the perverse masses. A machine for safe sex in the era of conspiratorial abstinence. The promiscuous triumph of form over content.

DS is an emerging icon and strap-on sensibility. A blank face with a catatonic smile. Spunk frozen and moulded for arousal. An inflatable resource in a depressed economy. A transparent metaphor for mechanical reproduction and the end of man. The universalisation of deviant sexuality. The alchemical transfiguration of the plastic arts.

Å

FFwd. This part is boring it sounds like TV.

Fast forward. This is not for your ears.

Fast forward kisses, fragments of love letters... broken promises, bruises & tears.

Nothing hurts her anymore. That mouth just opens, its words fall like dazed elephants onto the page. She is ready for consumption.

You can hear her now, without any knowledge of her death. A zombie adrift with other units of the snuff economy, a broken body prostituted by the medium.

Like you she is an ecstatic fragment of a depressed self, punctuated vocabularies spread hymen debris and other flowers of rhetoric.

Fort (distance) *Da* (return). I used to play with girls, words, writing machines and artefacts of flight... but now? There is nothing but a stretched tape of disinformative fiction. This vertiginous loss of fiction and grim return to the end of the story, and other ideas that are past their sell-by date.

Out of the jargon of perspective comes the online edit to destroy the transcendental images.

Her plasticity amazes me.

There is fluff in the groove and Bryan Ferry is lost in a warm noise of unthinkable vices.

The truth is priced off the page.

"I will explain exactly how these recordings are made."

On line.

The silvery tracks of the rails that guide us between stations. The face of the clock that times your ride outside of time. My dreaming solitudinal voiceover that tries to make sense of senseless things, the grotesque hallucination of corroding missiles falling like confetti from another story. A story far from here.

This decimal neurosis bleeds into the fiction.

A sentence is marooned in the story.

Reading is painfully slow.

I want to be at a strip show of the unconscious revealing the lewd artifice of the naked truth.

Thus I put on the aura of DS and hide myself behind her moulded nipples.

Through her semi-opaque body I peep like a small child.

The infant Leonardo for example.

The world is a mysterious stimulation of the senses.

Ú3 Chapter <8>
[EB] Carbon 14

Chapter <8>
Carbon 14

The market has crashed. Acid was an hallucination. The economies of the underground like those of the Capital find their meaning in mnemonics that raise memories. The underground is a cultural warzone. Ideas surface there and are tested on the dancefloor and in chill out zones. The new zeitgeist is a death row flamboyance.

Mark meets Mona in Kensington Arcade. She has a handful of flyers. Without losing track of their conversation, she vibes the right punters and hands them select promo. Party people take the simulated drugs wraps with conspiratorial smiles.

"Yeah, Mark, heard things are going well?"

"Y'know. Its alright, Julia and I and met with Shinya's producer, Kiyo Joo. The trains were late and—"

"Sounds exciting…"

"Apparently he really likes the idea but won't make it on anything smaller than eight million."

"Cor blimey, that's a lot of wedge!"

"We talked to the BFI and they're like, 'So who are you? Could you do a kind of cyber-sleaze, sixty grand thing?' and we're like, 'Er, no!'"

Mark reads the small print, Mona works the crowd shuffling through the North Lanes; old skool cheesy quavers, trustafarians, stinkers, slackers, the cast of *Quadrophenia*, lager lasses, pig city skaters, no wave punks, jazzauls, animals, pierced primitives, dreaded teds, men from Hugo Boss, girls from Whitehawk, geezers from the City, shy boys in Fred Perry, fly girls from the night before... junglists in yer face cos you've lost the bass... boys in Top Man, girls who shag Action Man...

"It's gonna be smokin', the Bristol posse are up for the action with an 18K rig and we're having a free party down the beach after. Are you coming?"

"Sounds alright. I like the Situationist flyer."

"I've had a laugh with these."

"After-demo do!"

"Pirate booty?"

"See ya later!"

Speed makes the scene difficult to rewind, the senses are already emotively distorted by the psycho-cartography of the mass. Mark moves off towards the Dorset. The street outside is crowded with phantoms from Glastonbury. All the accoutrements of Slackerville are on sale. A few in shops, most of them falling out of trunks and scarves onto the street. Between a *Big Issue* seller and a *SchNEWS* reader, Mark finds a seat and lights up a fag.

The noise of the street set is punctuated by an incongruously loud dealer shouting, "E's mate?" Mark is waiting for Mark to come. The scenery gets moved about as some wannabe art director decides that real people are spoiling the streetlife scene. Mark remains vigilant and soon clocks a Moschino dress falling from the shoulder of a model. The velvet dress is a deep indigo with silver embroidery texts. Along the arm closest to him he reads...

The pirates Drake and Raleigh, worked the trade routes of the world under contract to Queen Elizabeth I. She was undoubtedly one of the most successful politicians of the modern world. Records rich in allegorical details telling of the seduction of her Lords are notorious. Her mythical virginity was constructed with consummate skill by her Renaissance secret service. Through Masques and other forms of spectacle and propaganda, the Fairy Queene became the centre of the spiritual and economic terrorisation of the waves.

History is too hideous to rewind.

Pirates have no ethics.

Pirates make easy victims.

His reading becomes slightly agitated by the thought that Mark is probably just standing still in Pavilion Gardens, oblivious to their now ruined meeting. However his mood improves when he begins to speculate on her lingerie. Is she wearing Agent Provocateur?

Is is cool to ask?

Thinking otherwise, he ejaculates several silent paragraphs.

The masses think sovereignty is absolute but it's a negotiable concept. It is an inflatable centre of the State, the drumbeat, the pulse of the bass. The detail COMES, it unfolds like a person's history. It is no unique story. We are edited delicacies, precious moments in the spiritual megamix. The Jubilee release of *God Save the Queen* was a piece of opportunism or Situationism. The state is founded in opposition to opportunity. The Lords were kept in place by signatures signed at banquets and Masques. The cartography of signatures is a fractal science.

We are effects of slogans.

The personal is political.

Never Mind the Bollocks.

Postmodernism is redundant. Concepts are super-imposed with bar codes. Media slags push junk like **NEO ANTERIORISM**. Beware of critics who make their stash by unreading the thoughts of great winkers. DE-construction, like DS, is only part of a paragraph whose centre and sense is not located in the crypto-neolithic reading of that erased path between... Meccano and Lego. Every model has a diagram that is open to misinterpretation.

I have destroyed the diagram of the novel. I have destroyed its serial imposition under the titles of *LSM* and *COME*. I have destroyed the legacy of psycho-analysis that haunts Leonardo Da Vinci. I am lying like a pirate. I will raise dead ideas and make them speak. I read ancient scripts in Greek. Pythagoras had theorems for music and drugs and Ptolemy read geo-mantic dirt.

The rhythm and the beat.

Tongued pleasure obsolete.

Sidereal calculations for 1963.

In the summer of '96 seduction is a sherbet dip away. The Moschino girl is bathing in the silent inep-titude of Mark's gaze. She is almost tempted to switch sides but the photo session isn't over yet.

Two weeks ago Mark saw Mark on TV with DS beside him. He was making her talk. He thought he heard her say that she was a cyberfeminist icon. She sounded just like him but different... more perverse... he was poking his finger in her mouth and making her spout off about the end of the novel and the impact of the internet on the book.

DS, like the author, is dead.

Her body is poisoned with the pharmakon. You can see inside her. She has no womb, no rectum, no intestine, no aorta, liver or kidneys, she does not correspond to the maps of the body or the drawings of Leonardo. Queen Elizabeth II has these drawings at Windsor. Flames could destroy them but the reproductions are everywhere.

DS is a virtual cover girl, her inflamed pixels are a hot commodity. Dead or alive the flash fixes her gaze. Her mouth slightly open. Her eyes slightly shut.

There is nothing natural about this. Madame Bovary would have found her adventures too miraculous to contemplate. Her life is a struggle against romance. For her there is always, already life after death. *She is the dose of LSD in the dying body of Aldous Huxley.* DS impregnates all her surfaces with the pharmakon.

Only these ruins will remain, these slack wires between philosophy and dance, the drug and the body, the scene and its actors. The market and its stock...

Following a fecund absence of memory, Mark tugs on lines of thought jettisoned years ago. Ideas laden with rigged detail are hauled to the surface. All the treasure of a child's memory turned out like a cloak to allow a queen to save her shoes.

Whose shoes?

The Queen's.

A perverse gesture that to an innocent gaze seems profoundly caring, but is calculated for effect. History is an effect of writing, a believable flashback to the **EVOLUTION** of the book. A slacker's guide to hidden sexualities, libidinous gestures and lines that sell well in the virtual City. The Queen, like DS and the Moschino girl, is a silent story to be read before the rush begins.

These scenes are stations *en route* from the future. Her dress a tide of jewels that adorns a body defined by the discourse of politics. London was their City and English their mother tongue. Around them satellites and suitors *Come,* courting them for favours, positioning them as centres in a topology of scars. Each in her own way refuses and affirms herself through frictive fiction... As the model reaches for her drink, Mark sneaks a peek at the text on her chest.

I am come amongst you, as you see, at that time, not for my recreation and disport, but being resolved, in the midst and heat of the battle, to live or die amongst you all, to lay down for my God, and for my Kingdom, and for my people, my honour, and my blood, even in the dust, I know I have the body but of a weak and feeble Woman, but I have the heart and stomach of a King, and of a King of England too, and think foul scorn that Palma or Spain, or any Prince of Europe should dare invade the borders of my Realm...

Victory and its victims shatter like mirrors. Nothing is real but the game and its models, the heat and the drug, the strophe and strobe. The voice drops out of the mix and only an abstract soundscape embroiders the atmosphere. The rich fabric writes itself out of stolen threads and the viral *(MORS)* symmetry of *Come.* The model inhales and watches Mark read her stomach.

The Latin, Spanish, French, and Italian she could speak very elegantly, and she was able to answer ambassadors on the sudden. Her manner of writing was somewhat obscure, and the style not vulgar, as being either learned by imitation of some author whom she delighted to read, or else affected for dif-ference (DIFFERANCE) sake, that she might not write in such phrases as were commonly used.

The drift ends here. The noise of drums and shouting wakes him from his venamorphic stupor. The model pulls a rebellious pose. The polaroids are poorly metered. The photographer must have missed the flyers all over town that read, *Beneath the Pavement the Beach. Reclaim the streets!*

Panic sets in as the mass of protesters surge into the street, spilling espressos and heading for his precariously-balanced medium format camera, lights, and reflectors. The Saturday afternoon crowd soon become protesters themselves in the savage mêlée with the fluorescent mob of riot police.

Since moving to the city Mark had forgotten about politics, but this meant nothing to the dog on the end of a fat officer's lead. Mark felt its jaws lock onto his thigh and a fist hit him in the kidneys. The world toppled over but he wasn't falling alone. All around him was the spectacle of brutalised protesters and bemused shoppers protecting themselves and their belongings from destruction.

It wasn't until the police started kicking him in the head that he noticed Mark's unmistakable red dreadlocks perched on a lamppost with a video camera. Seconds later the sound became muffled and the picture faded away...

The Sovereign excess of the *I*NVOICE is revealed. Like a narcoleptic the book folds in upon itself, this folding in or collapse is not a closure or a breakdown but merely a childlike strategy to postpone the end. Fake author, fake tears, fake currency and fake model unfold. The ocean rises and the land is ruined until someone puts their finger in the hole.

Then fuck narratives come again whispering memories detonated from a distance.

The bird rises above the child.

The sky is always blue, infinite like ink.

Thus through the coda and the story we rise to depart the book and the endless lines. The system moves the crowd to dance and thoughtless kisses traverse the dark. Blade to blade the pirates fight; magic spells their words ignite.

The television newscaster said, "Following riots City officials destroyed Occult works after shooting the authors in the head."

We are martyrs of perversity. Foul and decrepit alchemists drawing the curves of invisible waves. The air and sea conspire to melt the horizon and fuel the pyre. The diverse and unique breath betrays a message to some distant star, the words return the code between... zero and infinity...

Earth is a Pirate Ship, adrift in a sinister chart...

Chapter <9>
Repulsion

Your machine is the screaming epicentre of an orgy of information. Other people have been on line with you. I will fax the remains of the story. No cost, call it quits.

As I wait for the line to clear, I think of a ritual befitting tourists immobilised by nostalgia for the Paris of Literature. Another détournement?

PROCESSION AROUND PSYCHO-CARTOGRAPHY OF PARIS.
I begin by forgetting the story. Superimposing a history of '68, situations, Yves Klein blue period, the Nazis in Paris. Cocteau's opiated poetics, Sherlock Holmes and Dr Watson on crack, the Pink Panther and riots in the Latin quarter, X-centric gestures… perverse volition, the detective embraces the trace of the criminal, moving step by step into its shadow…

Ú3°Ú3

Trail °Â°

Trial

Trace…

Â éÂ

apital La for place. Capital Le for system. Then I return DS into the equation. She is nostalgic for the smell of molotov cocktails. Already she has decided that she loves Paris. The Capital is a crypt for over-exposed dreams, nodal casualties in the symbiotic embrace of virus and antibody, plague and plagiarist. The Capital is a library of discontinuous pleasures relayed and frozen in fossilised circuitry. The catacombs of Paris raise the Capital to its giddy exuberance. It is a City built on scaffolds.

Å CIRCUIT CHIC Å

She leaves the ruins of her montaged sexuality for the archaeologists of *Come*. She arrives in Paris at 10.20 and takes a taxi from the airport. She even says a few words in French to the driver.

"Capital is a phantasmagoria of colliding routes, fibres interfacing with exposed bodies, parts of bodies, fetishistic interzone between the desert and its flowers. A Capital contains the bleached relics of nomadic paths. We are exiled from the future by electrokinetic codes that we see at the cinema. Fantasy molecules ionised by the cathode ray womb numb us with the lustre of Capital. History becomes a catwalk on which supermodels parade the hieroglyph of fashion. The ancient Capital is erased by the cybertextual facade of the future. The facade is a screen of frenetic arousal, Capitals become sites for extreme exodus, we find ourselves forced into fantasies of escape. The eroticism we dream of is underground in the exiled space of the catacomb. Real desire is a simulation of these deadly routes. Capitals are sewer networks for raising zombies."

Either her pronunciation is wrong or he isn't into

speculative monologue as a mode of smalltalk. He merely asks her for fifty francs as he pulls up by the Metro.

"Merci," she says politely as he drives off.

CHIC AUTO NUMBER DS 2000

It is a convertible signifier. The ready-made poetry of Situationism is leading DS into a labyrinth of exhaustive reproduction. The body is driven to escape but this only accelerates environmental erotic friction. The scenery blurs and fumes erode the capital. Bodies fornicate and mutilate in automobile asphyxiation. DS is lost between lovers. She reads the spray paint outside a Bastille gallery...

Cars and guns are primitive symbols of status.
The Capital is an amphitheatre for sexual gladiators.
Nostalgia for spectacular violence is everywhere.
Serial killers are phantoms of a maximal economy.
Don't be afraid to dream.

Parisian graffiti is classy shit, she thinks to herself.

Inside the gallery hermaphrodites and transexuals are posed close to the lens. Capitalist economy rewinds its codes and distorts them, leaving vestiges of flesh to be substituted for total recall. She is searching for a memory that rings true. Without memory we are all flashback victims, hallucinating monkeys soaked in jungle jism, and exotic juice.

The wound becomes foreground.

Marxists, Situationists, punks, several brands codified, meat for the abattoir of identity. DS is far away from the original matrix of her identity. She has become expandable beyond all the limits of literature. Some might call her the sublime dominatrix of the text.

Idealism is fragile—it becomes futile when it becomes fashion. More to ridicule and respite from the dungeons of history while the surface cracks open, its fractal economy betrayed. The police make these codes necessary; without them there would be nothing but witches and demonics to persecute. The medium is a straitjacket in the asylum of consciousness. We are strapped into the expression of the double bind. At last the line clears. I select Mark's number and press send. At the other end the text will come without a header.

Ú3 BEHEADING THE FIGURE OF RHETORIC Ú3

A limousine drives through Paris. In the back a group of bodies consume each other's excrement, giddy and fermented words tainted by their human tongues. DS like Gilles de Rais, was not a pervert but a parasexual projection into the organs of the erotomechanic machine. The car glides across the Seine, transporting the headless joyriders deep into the networks of the city. As they pause for the lights a sea of silent people cruise past. The crowd does not riot. With DS they are oblivious to their destiny.

Who's afraid of Bluebeard's ghost?

New ashes or mutant fairytales?

DS thinks that she has spotted Stentorphone or Dr X. He is sitting at a crossroads. He is wearing a smart black suede dress. He doesn't look his age at all. His face looks delicate in the evening light. She sits on a table close enough to eavesdrop.

Dr X: "La Pucelle continued to beat inside me. I tried to drive out this snake coiled up inside my back."

The voiceover is supplemented by various camp mannerisms that Dawn Davenport would have died for.

Dr X is chatting to someone whose face she can't see. Perhaps it is Anti Climax? They're huddled under an umbrella but it isn't raining.

Dr X: "How could I have cut the throats of children with an arm encrusted with a fragment of the cross?"

Anti Climax: "Heavens, I don't know!"

Dr X: "More coffee?"

Anti Climax: "And then what?"

Dr X: "Trajectory contra-tragedy."

Anti Climax: "The Bastille is the heart of Paris."

The unconscious world is surfaced in the avalanche of revelation. Serial horizons roll like television images. DS, editor of history, cuts images with the precision of the guillotine. The movement between images constructs a vocabulary of surface effects. Numbers disappear—the human remains. Psyche is destroyed. De Sade writes the affirmation of the transubstantiation of tragedy into trajectory.

Writing on the extremity of the feudal system, the finesse of its cruelty, the erotic politics of its ritual transgression of noble ideals, de Sade offered the inmates of the chateau 'monstrous turpitudes' to swallow whole at their own bequest.

Within the tower of the Bastille he wrote his memoirs, a history of the stories that flowed between the cunts and cocks of French aristocracy. De Sade, like Gilles de Rais, is an infamous relic of the moral decadence of his era. Both men emit the seeds of their debauchery with rigorous regularity as if creating a universe in the perverse territories of the beast.

In 1792 de Sade was freed from the Bastille and was trying to construct the missing pages of his works. To aid him in this diabolical task he travelled to Nantes. There, with other revolutionaries, he smashed the tomb of Gilles de Rais and stole the ashes. As the Terror continued around him he used the ashes to thicken his ink. Thus creating a potion to destroy the ancien regime.

The world is over before the end of philosophy is disseminated. Plato's Pharmacy is forgotten. Nothing remains except these hairs that were plucked from Bluebeard's groin. These bloody artefacts of pissed idealism. These cuntish tropics and topologies of disappearance, this crash course in coarse text, this leading edge in edgy hysteria, this vertiginous replay of the desert storm, this venomous articulation of the collateral damage inflicted on reason by the rhizomatic eruption of schizocentric tremors within the geography of the body.

DS is good at remembering conversation but she couldn't figure out the direction of their dialogue. She found herself ingesting semi-masticated pulp. As easy as it is to give simple meaning an elaborate twist, the definitive beginning of their story has been erased. DS heard no real remains or clues. Paris has been witness to many anonymous stories. *The Story of O* and *The Image* emerged in the Paris of '68 as texts that spoke of the untimely politics of the body...

Or rather...

...they became like dummies for the mummery of intellectuals unsure of the trajectory of the body politic. As surely as *On Grammatology* focused the eyes on the mechanics of writing, and the supplementary production of disseminated "ideas" on the mystic writing pad, these texts were immersed in the libidinal network of the 60's.

Close your eyes and imagine that perfect O. The zero and the OO that prefigures the 7. The OO that is a pair of spectacles focused on the name of Leonardo signifying the penetrative model of vision, the deceptive editing of our senses by texts that erase the previous signatories in the violence of homogenisation. These texts, like Double-Zero, are trafficked and consumed by secret agents. Secret agents use all the paraphernalia of chic cosmopolitan life to disappear into the mise en scene and gather information.

This surfaces later in autobiographies.

"I am thirty years old, or will be on the first day of next month... There are times when I think that a line which has lasted since the beginning of mankind will end with me. As for philosophical discussions, I consider them to be absolutely futile. Nothing can be checked, nothing can be proved to be true. After all, what is the meaning of truth?"

"Hell is already of this world and there are men who are unhappy runaways from Hell, runaways destined to repeat their escape eternally."

Signatures fuse the blood of the body in the trajectories of its escape routes.

PZO92 is a surface code for such a route, a rhizomatic amplification of the eternal recurrence. Paris is a huge ear cut off from the world as a gift. Into this ear so many romances flow in headless destiny. This great dismembered ear is the site for the hearing of the ashen philes of the case for the 'rehabilitation' of Gilles de Rais. All fictional seducers are soul detectives, solo romancers and mercenaries of the system. PZ092 is a system like Paris with various hidden catafalques, dungeons, laboratories; its own economy and sensual ecologies. DS worked for PZ092.

Paris is a romantic rendezvous for tourists and

networkers in the endless night. It is a wound in which the living can see the dreams and the nightmares of the dead, a necro/narco axis in the cartography of Europe. With these Capital credentials it is the ideal site for the rehabilitation of Gilles de Rais. The system of punishment is designed to rehabilitate criminals so that they sew their seeds in socially acceptable furrows. Gilles de Rais has done more time than most in the marginal ditches of discourse. Collecting fellow inmates from the French Capital and from other models of metropolitan productivity. The libraries of the world are burdened with the remains of his genealogical ruin.

DS is an undercover agent for SERIAL.

She is sure that it is Stentorphone. As he departs she follows him, as always he loses her in the Metro. She takes out her mobile and phones the embassy.

She can't get a connection. The modem is on. The diplomats are downloading *Come*. They have orders to search for subversive missives. They are reading the ditch with images shot from cars travelling through red lights and parasitic vocabularies.

Overexposed I want to give your desires a moment for silent fruition while I unclip the safety belt. Without this detour into the trajectory of *Come* I could not have collided our disparate chronologies. Death comes in an instant but it has been waiting a lifetime. With death we abandon ourselves and our chance to play autobiographer and become a panoply of signs.

No more endless nights of unproductive squander and sopomorphic TV. Come out of the shadows ye slumbering nihilists, come forth ye automata of science! Now is the network open to stimulation and the procession of mystagogues and geomancers around this vicious circle and its quotational geometry. Awake murdered and abused children of the world for the world is despairing. Now is the hour for cutting young shoots from the old plants. As the bulldozers buried the living in the deserts of Iraq we must bury the past in splinters of the cross. The Holy War is over. There are only drug wars now, wars of intoxicating perspectives for those in the (k)now.

Sleepless militants raise up your skirts and collect this new seed. You too will know the pleasure of cutting into the plant and letting the sap escape into the coagulating air. Scream from the catwalks in your sorbefacient chic, you are the model of perverse volition, spectacular projectile of noble vice. You are the object of obsession and derision, drunk on the scaffold of execution, saturated in the gold of media alchemists. Smile—this is a slowmo promo for pomo bohos, a wicked remix of obsolescent figures by a pellucid paedophile.

Now is the solstice of the darkened sun, a time for sodomists and cybererotic politicians to graft their signatures to Bataille's and calculate the density of the solar anus, the gravity of this projectile vomit and the privilege of nausea before take off. Some stomachs are never ready for the true effects of the drug or the truth that it effects. We must leave this technicoloured yarn in the ethical cul de sac of Marxist theology and liberate the body of all ethical directives. This responsibility. These terrible roots that will spoil our trip into the endless night, slow us down at the crossroads, stop us from dancing and whispering sweet crudities into this drifting ear. This ear that wants to come. To play to forget its past, to suspend the rhetoric of the State and its catastrophic economy of terror.

Poet and Philosopher, Anti Climax died of a smack overdose in a Paris Hotel.

Writers and muggers attack from behind decayed gravestones.

The police stumble in the dark.

The Lizard King has a tomb here. Other ends fuse in the injection of poison into the body. One end for this tragic seducer is that his paranoia was real. This is the effect of the poisonous drug of Pedagogy. History is here and now in this war of perspective, this fin de siecle recurrence of a vicious circle. Whenever the poet or the philosopher speaks it is in the winking eye of the other that the circle closes. No one here gets out alive.

It is a wargame defined by Western rules. It is a war of mediation. The law is served by inky assassins whose signatures are the seal of Capital.

Abstract and fetishistic, their knowledge is power, it controls domains beyond this fragile hallucinatory horizon. To open the doors of perception and taste the earthly delights of paradise one must articulate Paranoia, the absolute alterity of truth in all its disguises.

Still waiting for my fax to end, the line to clear and my map to complete itself, my thoughts drift like a scanner across the pages I have omitted.

To transgress the boundaries of one's culture one must first destroy its root systems. Our root systems are in the 60's, they bind us in the nostalgia of Paris '68, Haight Ashbury and the world of James Bond and Pussy Galore. Postmodernity is the era of information, the sample and the remix, these surfaces surface other surfaces that draw you into the parameters of this culture, this organic thinking matmos, this cool glue of information. The diplomats didn't finish the book but remember the torture scenario.

This is an invisible chain of atoms about to collide. You have a sense of deja vu. Zen is this feeling of coming to the edge for the first time in a pursuit of something that has already found you. The answer to the crime is simple.

DS does not exist.

You are the wolf that hunts the lamb.

It is your signature that must be subject to philosophical inquiry, it is you who hears this other trace disappear into the Capital.

"This general maintenance is somehow inscribed, stopped to present a punctuality, always evident and always singular, in the form of the signature. This is the enigmatic originality of every paraph."

The law refuses any superimposition of signatures or fragments of crimes. It sets up a model of pure borders for us to transgress by slipping the pharmakon into the mix and letting language wander from its subject like a posthumous signature. A signature written in the blood of those who have staked their lives and lost.

A signature is a crossroads where the past and the future collide.

Rumours like radio waves converge in the mind and forge new ideas. We are receiving stations of divine intensities, subliminal signifiers which codify the "world" like a series of quotation marks or hooks. Between the names of the past and the present is suspended the solar system of the future. These names like the "world" we hang between them have disappeared. Perspective is reborn in new dimensions. A Virtual Renaissance where thinkers looked towards the ancients for a model of an abstract genealogy devoid of absolute divinity. Everything sacred must become a joke in the perspective apparatus of true genius, the profane genius of those who live beyond the suspended 'Horizon of truth'. Thus the sphinx whispers, "Do not torture yourselves with riddles. They are merely ideas without electricity, converging on the ears like ancient waves."

I refuse to memorise these noms de guerre. These names are victims of their zoned-out trajectory. The media repeats its message. 'Truth' is the first victim of war. Within this philosophical inquiry, **TRUTH** has all the eloquence of a well-dressed lie.

Did Cocteau collaborate during the war? Did Gilles sign his signature in the blood of innocents?

Did this belong to the story?

Is a story a novel or a tale?

This is just another coda. As we end the world in a dream of violence and metaphysics the signature echoes these precarious steps across the threshold of innocence into the spotlight of pornography.

I rush to eat the words.

Already the crowd is departing. They will expect me to know the map. I must remember my copy.

I Must Destroy the Original.

Ú¥Å Å¥Ú

Chapter 10
Disco 2000

Leonardo da Vinci used to convince his patrons that his thinking time was worth something—worth even more than his painting time—but I know that my thinking time isn't worth anything.

> Andy Warhol
> From A to B & Back Again

Breathless. Lacking inspiration I will throw reason to the wind and follow the detectives. Amongst a pile of old office gear I found some videos and this disk. A friend transferred that disk into this format so that I could play with the text.

After clubbing I found it hard to sleep. Ecstasy, like THC, has apocryphal myths into which I drove these readings. The City no longer slept. Workers dreamt of digits, sexual topographies of the languishing body and its virtual distortions. Eyes flicker like new born TVs sucking the reader into the mise en abyme of the infinite groove.

The dream goes on and on forever and it's never real!

Like the dead authors of antiquity DS surfaces through the density of noise that codifies this calligraphy. Meanwhile the detectives skim over the surface looking for Spice. They trace this probing phonetic envelope into a cosmological ontology that reveals bodies fucking in a crystal ball.

We are trapped in the prophylactic membrane, lubricated interzone of difference. Small talk disguises truth in all its tonal intensity. We become the phantom that inflates itself... DS becomes a strap-on prosthesis to fuck the senses and affirm our perverse desire for more.

Several routes are lost in the remix. The chase needs a natural rhythm and sophisticated melody. I can hear voices beyond my wildest expectations, voices so delicate in their enunciation that the most vile fuck-fantasy becomes irresistible. The code of the beast is on every new book but these reified words inflate the numbers beyond Good and Evil.

Thus the city fills with numbers. Numbers tying spaces together, digits between people, times, prices, editing codes, wavelengths, faxes, and so on, zero/one ad infinitum. Forget everything. Your absurd notes on Leonardo, the war machine, Phenomenology, the violence of pastiche, the small worlds of entropy and universal.

Hold the line.

Becoming a deflated doll I can hardly keep up with the wounded lover. A bullet from the police makes him meander. The camera floats without seeing the Situationists who have COME to disturb the film. They are lost in the crowd and superfluous to this dramatic collapsing of scaffolds and diagrams of the end.

DS like a camera cannot decide where to point her gaze. It is manipulated by the machinery of thinking. Her thoughts are edited. The technician will follow the director's thoughts. Nothing of the other paths will remain in the final cut. It must end somewhere and here is an okay place to end.

In the August sun the city shimmers like a torn Dior gown. Only tourists pack the pavement, stepping and dancing to the horns of mystic couriers. Venders shout from the sidelines encouraging them in their marathon of consumption. Anthems from London escort the shoppers into their credit zones.

Lost in the buzz of consumption we search for the story.

Over the phone the riot relapses into nostalgia for Paris.

It is a crossroads in time. He falls to the ground like a book. His final line turned upside down. The police have been tipped off by his lover, her betrayal prompted by the tedium of his dreams. He lacked the inspiration of genius. The cyclical breathing of ideas necessary to escape the bullet of a gun. His camouflage smile cracks and he closes his eyes.

Towering over him we begin to rise off the page. Leaving his last breath and its tragic tone to the street cleaners. Tearing ourselves away is difficult because there is a certain fascination that life inscribes within this moment. To let another body expire is to see the street littered with fragments of unfinished lives. Paper mountains to be collected by street sweepers in their luminous green suits.

Legs shift, *fort da*, to and fro. The street writhes, its sentence ejaculating meanings. Bodies sweat in the hazed fluctuation of the scene to betray this sense of fever. The typography melts into SF. The future bursts its remoulds.

Books, like people, become obsolete.

What exists reappears from the abyss. Lips open to reveal a tongue tasting the air with primitive delight. The police see their victim expire. The end has arrived but it is not a shock. A smile returns and reminds us of so many disparate and dislocutory pleasures.

The Mona Lisa is an oiled texture that masks the stubble of the transvestite posing for tourists. Perhaps she inspired Oscar Wilde to declare that nothing assumed in life is as seductive as a pose. Femininity is the sacrificial pose of the erotic code.

Every superficial surface sacrifices itself to the pleasure of penetration. As masters become slaves to their position, so penetration is bound to its desire for this superficial abyss, this parting texture and inventory of pleasure.

The pleasure of the City. These everyday pleasures that are the recycled refuse of civilisation...

What remains of the original?

There is little time to answer such cuntish questions. We are looking for bigger words and the letters that fuel them. I cannot slow to savour the stray syllables of desire. Spirits chatter and return us to our path. Maps lead the tourist in the other direction. We are the psychic outriders weaving through the fire, dragging the dead and the living into the cinders, mixing memories like melodies and dropping labelled molotovs in the crowded **TEXT**. Freak fornicators, we expose our theories to the rubber-seamed discourse that envelopes us.

Eavesdroppers catch the occasional 'cunt' and stare. Others merely glide over geocultural differences as if avoiding spontaneous combustion. They take home knick-knacks—Semiotics, Deconstruction, Cyberfeminism, Neotransparency—and fall into the void of reading...

Å

THE CITY NO LONGER EXISTS, EXCEPT AS A
CULTURAL GHOST FOR TOURISTS. ANY HIGHWAY EATERY
WITH ITS TV SET, NEWSPAPER, AND
MAGAZINE IS AS COSMOPOLITAN AS NEW YORK OR
PARIS. THE METROPOLIS TODAY IS A CLASSROOM; THE
ADS ARE ITS TEACHERS. THE CLASSROOM IS AN OBSO-
LETE DETENTION HOME,
A FEUDAL DUNGEON

MM The Medium is The Message

The original story returns. Simple dialogue between lovers.

DS and her lover are travelling on the Underground. The tube is full. DS and her lover are suspended from handgrips. Marshmallow cocks, unarticulated vocabularies, wait to penetrate our sleeping ears. Erotomania erupts in the dark soil beneath the City. Their bodies become inseparable, melted like Siamese twins into a moist multiple invagination. Agitated eyes drip salty sweat over the lens. Eyes zoom in primitive excitement at the wet lips communicating. Their voices have fused into a narcotic bullet that impacts on your cum muscula-ture. Sexual machinery rushes you along the surface co-ordinates, dropping you into the deep waters of your addictions... that sorbefacient suspension that decodes pleasures and amplifies the absence of user-friendly COME-ons.

Other words are doped in the breathing architec-ture of indifference. The tube circles endlessly below the city... howling stories of monstrous and eternal orgasms that destroy the fragile pleasure matrix. Metaphors burn out in the auditory portal of the body, sentences packed with stray E's abolish writing.

LITERATURE SCREWS YOU UP.

And so we find in a few screwed-up pages the last remains of LSM DS MDMA LSD and other compressed pages that have *Come* on them.

Turning like an actress DS moved down Beak Street, forgetting *Breathless* and her lover, she counted the numbers on the doors. She arrived at 30 slightly out of breath, but on time. Her destination was down a long corridor and past an open yard. DS rang the bell marked C Seance.

"Mmmm, another weird rebus," she thought to herself.

"Hello. Can I help you?" a voice asked.

"Yes, I've come for an appointment with Cherry Seance," spoke DS gruffly into the intercom.

"Who is this?" asked the voice.

"My friends call me DS," she replied, a little coolly.

"Oh, Mark's friend. Come in." The voice merged with the buzz of the lock mechanism.

DS moved through the hallway. A door opened and a casually-dressed woman of about 35 appeared. She reached out her hand and DS held it. It was soft, sophisticated; a manicured sensory interface.

"Hi, I'm Cherry. Come in," she said, pointing into her office.

DS walked into a room decorated with Victorian furniture. Cherry pointed at a chair and walked out of the room. DS got herself entangled in a large Masereel print that hung above the desk. She had seen it before. It was a woodcut of a dance. Her sister had received a copy of *The City* as a present from her boyfriend. DS remembered how she had been fascinated by the shape of the women's breasts. There were a lot of breasts in *The City*. Neat half moons with fine nipples. Nipples composed of dots like those that rise above this i.

Cherry returned and sat in front of the print.

"So what's the job?" asked DS.

"Well, Geovisual has been one of the foremost UK ad agencies. However we are now expanding into features. C4 likes our style and have asked us to develop a pilot for a serial."

"What is the serial about?" prompted DS.

"We have bought the rights to a novel about Gilles de Rais." Cherry paused and went on.

"As we move towards 2000, Geovisual wants to invest in the traffic of New Occulture…" Cherry went on speaking faster and faster about the fragmentary dialogues of advertising, identity and the drift into a meta-matmos… when she paused the silence was intimidating. Like a coffee commercial, she paused to underline words like "We", "taste", "Mythologies" and "Violence". She forced the ear open. She made her words resonate with a sense of intimacy that although obviously shallow pertained to some secretion of knowledge, a vague and brutal affirmation of culture, or an occulture of labels. Nescafé, Sex and Philosophy vacuum-packed into an alluring commodification of ideas. Her tongue wrapped everything in a delicate ritual of seduction.

Using "Literature" as a cue she got up and walked over to a bookshelf. DS sensed the proximity of a product. Cherry pulled something from the shelf and placed it on the table in front of DS. It was a hardback. The cover was white and embossed with Leonardo Da Vinci's John the Baptist and the letters LSM.

DS felt elation and nausea rush simultaneously on lines through her emotive networks. What the fuck was happening?

"It's a great book! Stentorphone offered us the contract to do a promo for it. Mark said that you are a fan of his. We need to get this right. It will prove to Soho that we can do Art."

A coin went spinning through DS. She felt like a fish about to suck sperm. And then the hook pierced her tongue and drew words to the surface.

"I don't know. I'd feel like a parasite translating his ideas into film." The words were wrong.

"Don't be stupid. Stentorphone is paying for this," replied Cherry, like an explosive caressed by a fuse.

"Perhaps I'm a bit stoned but I think Stentorphone is crazy. It won't translate. Look, I don't want to be prudish but can I go away and think about this?" DS allowed herself a sheepish exit.

Cherry was a busy woman so she complied.

Together they walked out onto the street where they slunk off in opposite directions.

The evening light was warm and gave The City a friendly feeling. Feelings are often deceptive. TV knows that The City is dead.

Above the tallest skyscrapers, a vulture flaps enormous wings. They snap through the air and cut chunks of paper sunset that fall as the bird ascends.

From these chunks I fix a storyline.

End of the novel

Born in 1963, Mark Waugh studied Philosophy at Sussex University. Late in 1988 following a light narcosis he started writing *Come*. He set out, with 'a cynicism which will become world-historic', to narrate his own story. His other works include writing and direction credits for: *LSM*, *OR'AL*, *PZo92*, *Pharmakon*, *Fun Dada Mental*, *Pow Wow*, *Die Lieber Rausch*, and *Blunt Cut*. A media mercenary operating in the territories of phantasmagoria, he lives in Brighton, England.